"YOU'RE IN TROUBLE, HERO—

YOU'RE IN A JAM!"

Click.
Gone.
Phone call from a stranger.
The phone call didn't even tell Barney
Glines what kind of jam it was—but he knew
they were after him, all right, and he knew
that what they wanted was blood—his
blood. . . .

*"Don't be a wise guy," they told him, "you
might get killed—"*

And even after he knew why they wanted
him, he couldn't be sure who'd have the
gun. . . . or the knife. . . . or the needle
. . . . meant for him—

It might be Gloria, the hopped-up dancer,
or it might be the cold sadistic killer known
as Frankie. . . . or it might even be the girl
with the sultry green eyes . . .

You'll Get Yours

by
Thomas Wills

WILDSIDE PRESS

You'll Get Yours

ONE

I LIE on the bed in my shorts, my legs spread-eagle, the back of my head resting on my hands to keep it from the soaking pillow. The window is shut and the blinds are drawn, just as I found them, and it is very hot.

I have not moved for the past hour, not since five minutes after I slipped into the room past the dozing Mexican clerk in the shabby little foyer below. Not even to light a cigarette. I even breathe through my mouth.

Next door it is not so quiet. The bottle clinks against the edge of the glass. Then the bottle thumps heavily on the table top. There is no rattle of ice. Ice? In this god-forsaken hole?

He has been at it since I arrived, and for who knows how many hours and days and weeks before.

Drink hearty, Archie. Down the hatch, kid. Bottoms up, you son of a bitch, you're drinking your last.

It has been getting dark in a hurry. When the sun goes down in little Tia Rosa, it sinks.

Tia Rosa, end of the line.

I swing my legs slowly to the floor and stand up. The outline of my body remains on the sheet, a silhouette in sweat. It is time for the blood. Archie St. George's. The tears? They've all been shed back in New York. By three beautiful women.

Back to the chair, to my tourist suit; white palm beach jacket and trousers, brown-and-white shoes, white shirt opened at the neck, white panama hat. I dress silently and unhurriedly.

A cough sounds through the cracked, paper-thin partition. A hacking cough. Too much tobacco, too much cheap whiskey, too much everything. That's all right, Archie. Dr. Glines is right next door. He's got the prescription for that cough, kid. I buckled the holster to my chest, went back to the bed and got the .38 from beneath the pillow. This'll fix that cough.

I pull the blind away from the window. The narrow dusty road beneath the window is no longer yellow but black. The shack across the street is not white any more. The only sign of life in the village is on the corner. There a dim light flickers. That's *La Cantada*, the local ginmill.

I'm not worried about that. When I leave I'll be heading in the opposite direction. My car is in a lean-to four blocks away. In an hour I'll be back in Brownsville, USA, and heading north again. Maybe Archie will come home again, too. In a baggage car, in a steel box with Railway Express stickers all over it. Addressed to me, maybe.

Okay, Archie. Drink up. I can't wait to see your face.

I had my fingers on the knob of the door that connects the rooms when the heels clicked in the hallway outside. I took my hand away.

It couldn't be her. But who else walks like that? The steps slowed. They were cautious now. They passed my door and then stopped.

There was a light knock on his door. Then a voice.

"Archie? Are you in there, Archie?"

It was her. I found myself staring at my hands. They were fists, shaking fists. I felt rage knotting my forearms, tightening my chest.

He didn't answer. I heard him cross the room unsteadily. He opened the door to her.

"What the hell are you doing here?" he said. The liquor was strong in him.

"I want to come in," she said.

"Why?"

"Let me in, Archie." Her voice was on hands and knees.

"Why sure, baby. Sure. For you, anytime."

The door closed. There was silence. I knew exactly how she would walk inside, then stop and look around at the cheap, dingy room. I could see him, too, standing near the door, leaning against it with his shoulders, going over her with his brown eyes.

Archie said, "Okay. Now what?"

"How long have you been here, Archie?"

"Too goddamned long." His voice was thick; surly and thick. There wasn't a trace of the old smoothness left. "I hope you brought money, baby, 'cause I'm coming back."

"Are you?"

"You bet your life I'm coming back."

"What about Barney?"

He laughed. "Barney? You think I'm down here on account of Barney?"

"He's looking for you, Archie. He's going to kill you."

He laughed again.

"It isn't anything to laugh at," she told him.

"Sure it is. It's the yak of the year, baby. Barney Glines is a goddamned boy scout. And you. You know what you are? A goddamned girl scout." His voice toughened. "What the hell'd you come down here for anyhow?"

"What do you think, Archie?"

"I thought you and me were all washed up, baby. Out of sight out of mind, they always say."

"It didn't work out that way, Archie."

"So I see. I didn't think I'd made that much impression." His voice was a leer.

Hers was soft and beguiling. "But you did. You made a very big impression, Archie."

"How'd you follow me, baby?"

"It wasn't easy."

I'll say it wasn't. It had taken me three long weeks to get to him. I had to give her credit.

She said, "But I'm here now."

"In the flesh," he said. "How's about a little drink, baby? To celebrate?"

"All right."

The bottle touched two glasses.

"Got to take it straight," he told her. "This isn't the Waldorf."

"Or the Park East."

That got a chuckle out of him. "No," he said, "it's not even the Park East. Here's to you, baby."

"Here's to you, Archie."

A pause. When he spoke again I knew he was next to her. His voice was deep in his throat.

"You look awful good."

"I feel good, Archie. Now that I'm here."

"No hard feelings, kid?"

Another silence. Maybe his arm was around her waist. The arm with the restless fingers.

"Drink your drink, Archie."

He laughed. "In a hurry?" he asked.

"Yes. A big hurry."

"Can't keep a lady waiting." I heard his glass come down hard on the table. "Take 'em off, baby."

She didn't say anything. It was worse than if she'd spoken. I backed away from the wall as though I'd been slugged. From the other room came scattered sounds, some of them indistinct, some of them I could label. She had taken her shoes off, for the soft thumping beats on the floor were her stockinged feet padding to the chair. She liked to wear suits. Maybe now she was laying her jacket neatly across the back of the chair. Then the skirt would be unhooked and slipped down over her hips. She'd fold it carefully.

"Put out the light, Archie."

"I like the light on. I like to look at you."

"Please," she said. "Please put it out."

He knocked the glass from the table and swore drunkenly. I heard him flick the wall switch. Then a soft thud that I couldn't identify.

Then his voice. "Come here, baby! Com'*ere!*"

I closed my eyes. That made it worse. I could see her

walking toward him, her head back, a smile on her beautiful lips. It was dark in there, but there was white light behind my eyes.

The cheap bedsprings creaked. She was in his arms. In his arms . . .

"You're the best," he said. He was very drunk. Not just tight anymore, but drunk. I knew why.

"Am I the best, Archie?"

"You always were. Those other two . . ." He stopped speaking.

"What about them?"

"They're just women." His voice was muffled. "You're the princess."

"We're all just women, Archie. All three of us."

There were no more words after that. Just sounds. The sound of the bed, the sound of movement, the sounds from his throat. Nothing from her. She was quiet. She generally was. Not always, though. There had been a night, a long night in New York.

But he made sounds. Moans. Then he made a particular moan—but I only heard the beginning of it. My hands were gripping the edge of the bed and something merciful flooded my brain, drowning out all sound. I couldn't have stood it otherwise. I'd have opened the door and killed them both.

After a while the roaring was gone from my head. It was over in there. It had been quick. Archie had been too full of liquor, too exhausted from months of hard riding on a trail that was downhill all the way. He had probably passed out.

All I could hear now was her dressing. She seemed to be moving around quickly, and stumbling into things. Why the hell didn't she turn the light on? What was there to be so modest about now? Maybe she didn't want to see herself in the bureau mirror. That might remind her of me, and of all that had happened in New York. Maybe she was as disgusted with herself as I was.

Her heels were clicking toward the door. It opened

and she went out, walking fast past my door and out of the little hotel.

I moved to the window. She came out and stood in the overhead light for a moment before turning in the direction of *La Cantada*. She wore a two-piece green suit and a large-brimmed white hat. Her legs were as long and as beautiful as they'd always been. Her figure still stopped the beat of my heart. I loved her as much as I had before she'd gone to his room.

She passed the bar and kept going. For a moment she was swallowed by the darkness. Then two red taillights blinked on. They moved away from the curb and faded out of sight down the narrow road.

I felt suddenly empty, all life sucked out of me. I had come down here with good reason to kill Archie St. George—for what he had done to her.

But apparently I was the only one it made any difference to. She'd certainly shown me how it was on her part. Then I knew that if I wasn't going to kill him for her, I was going to do it for myself.

I walked to the door, making a lot of noise about it, hoping that he'd hear me and be waiting with a gun in his hand. That's how I wanted it to be now. There was nothing to be careful about anymore, nothing to go back to.

I pulled the door open. It was pitchdark and I stood for a moment in the doorway, a dark target but a target nevertheless if he had guts left for a fight.

His body took form on the bed. He was sprawled on his stomach, out cold. I went and snapped the light switch. His head was sideways on the pillow, facing me. The face was still good looking, still tough looking, even with the mouth open and the lips slack. You couldn't take that away from Archie. He was a son of a bitch, but he was a handsome son of a bitch.

Then I found out you could take it away from him. There was a splash of red on the sheet, widening out from beneath his body even as I stared at it. I put my hand beneath his shoulder and raised him. Then I turned him completely on his back. Sticking between two ribs was a knife, a knife I'd seen once before. Its shaft pointed downward and its long thin blade had to be in his heart from an angle as sharp as that.

I pulled it loose. I lifted an end of the sheet, wiped it clean and dropped it in my inside jacket pocket. Then I looked around the room. Beneath the chair was her compact. That was the soft thud I'd heard. She'd gotten the knife out of her purse as soon as he'd turned the light out. The compact had slipped to the floor. Either she hadn't heard it or had forgotten about it as she dressed in the dark and left. I put it beside the knife.

I spent two more minutes wiping surfaces with my handkerchief. Chair, bureau, bed, doorknob—anything she might have touched.

Then I gave them a mystery. I locked his hall door and moved the bureau in front of it. I took the key to the adjoining door—which had been on my side—and tied a length of thread from the spool in my pocket to the end of it. I passed the thread through the old-style keyhole, closed the door from my side, relocked the door with my skeleton and then pulled the key up into the lock. When it was in place, its handle on his side, I slit the slipknot in the thread.

I take nothing from the Mexican police, local or national. But they would have a good time with a dead man in a room locked securely from both sides and with no access to the second floor window.

Then I got the hell out of there. Fast.

TWO

"BARNEY," he said, "meet Kyle Shannon."

It was a pleasure to meet Kyle Shannon, even though it was through Archie St. George; even though he stood with his hands on the back of her chair, fingers all but touching her slender neck; even though the eyes which she could not see were asking me: How'd you like a night with this, kid? How'd you like it?

I dropped my glance to hers. She would be tall when she stood up. Her face was an angular heart, rounded only at the chin. She had a small, razor-thin nose that flared suddenly above a glistening, good-humored, very sensuous mouth. Her hair was auburn, a reddish-blonde that hung to her shoulders and glinted warmly even in the artificial white light of St. George's office.

She wore a flannel dress as brilliantly green as her eyes, a dress whose high neckline only emphasized two very full breasts and each ripe curve of her body. She was my most beautiful girl in the world. That's all it takes, ever. When she is you know it in ten seconds. And from then on you hate every other man in the world who wants her.

"You're going to be hearing a lot about Kyle," Archie St. George was saying and I looked at him. But he hadn't been reading my mind. He was using his agent's voice, *Archie St. George, Artist's Representative.* He was giving me the buildup for her benefit.

He might have been wasting his time. Kyle Shannon sat rigidly in the chair, as though she wanted to get out of it and away from here. Her eyes, after their brief,

14

cool glance at me, were now directed beyond me, toward the door.

He was still talking. "Kyle's just come back from the coast," he said. "Her first picture."

That made more sense than most things they do out there. Our glances met again and I began to wonder why she disliked me so much. But she did.

". . . I don't know how much experience you've had with the industry, Barney . . ."

"None."

He nodded. "A first picture is a very delicate thing," he told me. "Especially now. Every studio is desperate for a new face, a new star. They have to have another Clark Gable, another Jean Harlow." He paused and his hands cupped her shoulders and tightened familiarly. "Some very important people," he said, "think they have one. The screenings of Kyle's picture are exciting, Barney. Very exciting."

I was watching his fingers. They were probing, probing, dissolving the material of the dress and I could see her nakedness flowing up into them, into his own body.

". . . of course," he was telling me, "the only payoff is the public itself. All a producer can do is put a girl in a picture. The people have to make her a star."

She had not moved for some time. Now, negligently, she raised her arms and lifted his hands from her shoulders.

"Can't we get to the point?" she asked. It was the first time I'd heard her voice. It was a vibrant sound, low register, coming not from her throat but from some musical box deep inside her chest.

I found him looking down at the top of her head with a face gone suddenly tough. He said, "I want Barney to have the picture, honey. The whole picture. He's a very particular guy."

His voice seemed to affect her. She lowered her head and began staring at her hands in her lap.

"Like I say," St. George went on, "a first picture is

a very delicate thing. It's got to be handled. The publicity story on Kyle, the angle, is the Cinderella thing. Kyle," he said, "was a fashion model. Lingerie, stockings, nightgowns, bathing suits—you know the stuff. The story on Kyle is that a producer happened to be leafing through *Vogue* and came across this nylon ad. Just a leg against a background of black velvet. He immediately sent a wire to the New York office to track that model down. The ad was traced to Kyle and a dozen pictures of her were rushed to the coast." He took a breath. "As the story will read in the magazines and the columns, this producer was even more impressed with the face than he was with the legs. He sent for her and signed her to a contract immediately. That's the story."

If what he was saying was a little rough it didn't seem to bother her. Her face was expressionless.

"The trouble is," said Archie, "Miss Shannon is not quite Cinderella."

"Can't we skip that?" she asked.

That made him laugh. "Not with Barney Glines," he told her, unasked for. "It's nothing to be ashamed of." He smiled across the room at me. "Miss Shannon has the tough luck of being a very, *very* rich girl. How much did your father leave you, honey?"

She said nothing.

"Kyle's father," he said to me, "was W. R. Shannon. If you're behind on your history, W. R. Shannon discovered how to separate aluminum from rocks. It pays better than getting gold out of rocks."

I was getting as fed up with Archie St. George as she was. "So what?" I asked.

"So that Kyle might not appeal to the public if she's already filthy with the stuff. The public reserves the right to make movie stars rich. It's bad form for Cinderella or Horatio Alger to start off with more in the bank than they could possibly earn."

"So what?" I asked again and I found her looking me

over. Not a thaw, understand. But some of the ice had chipped off.

"The cat might be getting out of the bag," the agent said. "Kyle checked into the Park East Hotel last Saturday. Last night her rooms were robbed."

"That's too bad," I said, but I might just as well have said nothing.

"It's *very* bad," St. George said. "They took a jewel case full of diamonds. A hundred thousand dollars' worth."

He was looking at me. I was looking at her. She was studying the tips of her fingers. "Who's the insurance company?"

St. George left his place behind her chair and walked slowly to the gaudy desk he kept. He lowered himself into an over-stuffed, mohair-covered swivel. "That's the problem, Barney. Kyle has the stuff insured, naturally. But she feels she doesn't want to file a claim."

"She does?"

"A claim," he said, fingering a cigarette lighter, "means police. Police mean newspapers. I think you can imagine how the *News* would love to have Kyle on their front page. Along with the lush details of her suite at the hotel and the sables and minks. Somebody," he said, "might even connect her with *the* Shannons. And all those stories her studio has carefully planted will look a little ridiculous. The bubble will burst and Kyle will be in the middle."

"Oh," I said and turned to her. "And the idea is to have somebody get your stuff back without any excitement."

"Yes," she said dully. "That's the idea."

"Well," said Archie, his voice bright, "what do you say, Barney?"

"I'll give it a whirl. The insurance company won't like it, neither will the police. But I'll try it."

I don't know what it was, but the more I said to this girl the less progress I made. The green eyes that raked my face were sarcastic now—if that's the word.

"Fine," St. George said. "I knew we could count on you, kid . . ."

"Don't expect a miracle," I said. "And don't expect anything overnight."

Archie St. George was smiling at me. "As a matter of fact, Barney, it's going to be a lot simpler than most of your jobs."

"In what way?"

"Kyle's been in contact with the thieves," he said.

"When?" I asked her.

"At three o'clock this morning." She said it accusingly. "Ten minutes after I'd discovered the theft."

"Kyle and I were at the theatre last night," St. George explained. "We dropped into the Stork for an hour or two and then I took her home. We had a nightcap and I left. When I got back to my place Kyle called me. She'd found the case missing from a drawer in the vanity. Then she got this call."

"What was said?" I asked her again.

"Not much," she answered. "The man on the wire told me he had my diamonds. He said I could have them back"—her eyes plunged into mine—"if I got in touch with Barney Glines."

I don't know how long I just sat there, I don't know what kind of expression I had on my face. I do know it was completely silent in Archie St. George's office. And I do know she had been given a hell of a fine reason not to like me.

Archie coughed and the spell was broken.

"How," I asked her, "would getting in touch with me help you? Did this man on the phone explain that?"

"He said 'Barney Glines' and hung up. Then I called Archie. He said you were a private detective . . ."

"I said you were the lad all the insurance companies hired," St. George interrupted. "I said . . ."

"Did you say that I wouldn't touch the ransom racket?"

St. George shrugged. His handsome face was bland. "Kyle's in trouble," he said smoothly. "She's my client and

she wants her jewelry back without any splash. She asked
me to get you over here, Barney. That's all I can do about
it." He stood up, got out a cigarette case and walked to
her. She shook her head and he lit one for himself.

"Well?" he asked. "What about it?"

Kyle Shannon was watching me and I knew she hadn't
changed her mind about me as a bag-man for some mob.
I could convince her by standing up, grabbing my hat
and walking out. That would leave me wondering why
some punk thief thought he could drop my name into
his lousy arrangements. It's fine to be a boy scout, but
only when you're twelve years old.

"How is it supposed to work?" I asked her.

"You mean you're in?" said St. George.

"I'm in," I agreed. "What am I supposed to do?"

"Don't you know?" the girl asked, her voice cynical.

I sighed. "As naive as it sounds, no, I don't."

Archie said, "I imagine they'll call Kyle again. She'll
tell them it's all set and they'll contact you. Wouldn't you
say that's how it works?"

I stood up. "Yeh. I'd say that's how it works." I took
my hat from the tree in the corner. "When I hear I'll
give you the word."

"Better call me, kid," Archie said. "I'll take care of
everything from Kyle's end."

It was nicely put. He was her agent. That made me the
mob's. I left his office and walked across town to my own.

THREE

THE DOOR reads: *Barney Glines, Investigations* in two neat lines. The door opens on an office ten feet by fifteen feet at sixty cents a square foot in a building that's been just west of Madison Avenue on 49th Street for the last thirty-five years. That makes it four years older than me but some mornings I wonder.

I opened the door and went over to the desk. I sat down and looked hard at the telephone.

"Ring, you son of a bitch," I told it.

The telephone rang.

"Glines?"

"Yeh."

"There's something for you at the desk of the Leewood Hotel. That's 45th off Broadway."

The receiver clicked softly and he was gone. See? It's simple. Why does everybody think it's hard to make a million dollars in this business? All you have to do is open an office and pay your telephone bills. And do things that make your stomach crawl.

I told the hackie that took me to the Leewood Hotel to wait. I walked into a foyer that held four chairs, a couch, a table, a sand-filled urn for butts and a seedy, threadbare rug that had been an ugly red fifteen years ago.

On the couch sat a sailor and a Broadway chippie who couldn't have been fifteen and could have been twelve. On one of the chairs was an old man studying the Green Sheet before he donated two more bucks to a bookie. On another chair was a bookie. On the third was a whore who got her legs crossed and uncrossed twice in the time it took me to pass her. The fourth chair held a hatchet-faced character who stared through my beltline from beneath his pearl gray Adam with the upturned brim.

The thing to do, of course, was to pick him up, carry him into the john and bounce him around until he came up with the right answers. That's the way I used to play this game. But this was a different league with different ground rules. And a girl named Kyle Shannon.

The desk clerk was a third-stage consumptive. Sick eyes turned to me vacantly out of a face that was little more than a transparent covering for his skull.

"Is there something here for Barney Glines?" I asked him softly.

He seemed to be thinking it over, getting the words in place. "You got some identification?"

I gave him a card that had my name on one side and my picture and thumb print on the other. He held it on the tips of his fingers and turned it backward and forward. Then he reached under the desk and handed me an envelope.

He moved away from me quickly as I tore it open and read the brief note. This was the jungle, and none of the cats was curious.

"Go sit in the lefthand phone booth," was the message.

Silly? For you and me, maybe, but not for them. They wanted a look at me, for one thing. That's so they'd know me if anything went wrong. Chances are I had even been photographed by this time. They also wanted me out of my office and on a phone they knew wasn't tapped— at least not tapped by me. There was also the psychology of having me jump every time they said jump.

I went to the lefthand booth, closed the door, sat down, lit a cigarette and waited. It took five minutes for the phone to ring.

"I'll give it to you once, Glines, so open your ears. Get twenty grand. Twenty. Small bills. Nothing higher than a twenty. Twenty tops. Put it in a briefcase. A black briefcase. Check the briefcase in the Long Island Terminal at Penn Station. Long Island Terminal, Penn Station. Put the check in an air mail envelope. Air mail. Leave the envelope with the night clerk of the Hotel Barnet. Night clerk. Barnet. 33rd and Seventh. Pick up the envelope he will have for you." He stopped the monologue for a brief pause. He said, "Don't be a wise guy. You'll get killed, Mr. Glines."

Click. Gone. Phone call from a stranger. So was hatchetface gone from his spot in the lobby. But that had been a stupid play. I'd pick out that punk again from the thousands who looked just like him. And take him off the junk for three hours, let him miss just one needle, and he'd spill his guts until you had to shut him off. That would be when Kyle Shannon had her stuff back and I was on my own again.

I got in the cab and we started on the long, long trip back across town. Three avenues and four streets. It would take twenty-five minutes, if we were lucky.

"The guy in the white hat," I said to the cabbie. "The thin one."

He lifted his head. "What about him?"

"Did he keep walking when he left the hotel or get in a car?"

"Car," said the cabbie. "Fifty-six Caddy. Black job with four doors." He swerved on Broadway to miss another cab and cut across a bus for his turn on 46th.

"New York plate?" I asked him.

"Yeh. But don't ask me the number. I don't play 'em."

That was too bad. Most of them do try to hit the numbers. Those that play memorize every license they see and they can read it back to you for five minutes afterward. Too bad but not hopeless. This was February and I doubted if delivery had been made on more than 300 Cadillacs in New York. That made it not more than 50 painted black and less than 25 of those would be four-door sedans.

This mob could be had. But who said thieves were smart?

All I got from the phone in Archie St. George's office was a busy signal. He uses about eight-hundred square feet—foyer, reception room, office—in a spanking new, steel-and-concrete, air-conditioned giant at 53rd and Sixth. If the nut is less than four hundred a month I'm surprised. But then, he's an *Artist's Representative* and works for his money. I walked over.

But the reception room was empty. Empty, even, of the receptionist who had been there an hour ago. A blonde, about nineteen or twenty, whose bosom performed at a ridiculous angle that confessed *Made on 34th Street*. But not a bad looking girl. They never were around Archie.

I forget whether I knocked on the door or not. But when I opened it I was met by the sight of the blonde, lying facedown on the couch, her black dress hiked above her stocking tops and her upper body shaking with sobs that even the cushion couldn't muffle. Archie St. George sat on the edge of the desk, a leg dangling, a cigarette between his lips.

We looked at each other for a moment. "All work and no play," I told him.

"See me later, Barney." His thin, high-cheekboned face was not its suave self but tightened and white with anger. And for the first time I was looking at his ink-black hair when it was not sharply brushed. It even looked as though somebody had gotten her hands into it and clawed.

"I'm seeing you now."

The girl had begun to lift her head at the first sound of my voice. Now, still crying uncontrollably, she swung herself untidily to her feet. On her left cheek was an ugly red welt.

I took her arm. "You better sit down a while," I advised her.

"Why don't you butt out, Barney?"

"What happened to your face?" I asked her.

She shook her head. "Nothing," she whispered. "It's all right." She moved around me and left the office.

"If you need a workout," I said to him, "why don't you try the gym over on 52nd?"

He took a deep drag of his cigarette. "Let me work out my own little problems, hanh? My dames are not your worry."

He had me there.

He said, "You turn up anything on the diamonds?"

I sat down on the couch. "Her stuff is going to cost somebody twenty grand."

He shrugged. "Steep," he said. "But cheap, considering."

"Considering what?"

He snubbed the butt in a tray. "Considering Kyle Shannon," he said. "That picture she's made is really good. The studio is talking in terms of 4-million gross." He smiled briefly. "Twenty thousand is money to us. But not stacked against 4-million. How do they want it handled?"

I told him.

He listened carefully and then he nodded. "The envelope you get will probably have another check in it. Or a key to a box in Grand Central or LaGuardia."

"In that case," I said, "all I should do is pick up my envelope first."

He smiled. "Sure," he said. "Do that, Barney. I'll send flowers."

"Nothing would happen to me."

He spread his hands and when he spoke his voice was bored. "You're the expert," he said. "My only angle is to protect Kyle. If you get yourself killed I'll just have to start all over with a new boy."

"That would be an inconvenience," I admitted.

He ran his fingers through his hair. "Why don't you just play it smart, kid? Make the payoff and make the pickup. Okay?"

"Okay."

"About twenty grand. I'll get that from Kyle tonight."

"I can get it," I said.

He shook his head. "That's another thing, Barney. The girl."

"What about the girl?"

"Private property. Strictly. I just thought I'd warn you."

I grinned. "You know what you can do with your warnings."

"Don't, Barney," he said. "I'd kill you over Kyle Shannon."

Well, you have to expect days like these. But you don't have to keep taking it. I got up and went over to him. My fingers wrapped themselves around the big knot in his tie and I pulled him closer.

"Agent," I told him, "you keep saying things like that and you're going to get knocked silly."

"Let go, Barney." His voice was thin. "I can't take being handled. Take your goddamned hand off me!"

I didn't hit him and be done with it. I don't know why. I just spun him away from the desk and shoved him away from me.

"Get the money!" I shouted at him. "Get it and then get out of this thing. The more I see you the more I want to take you apart."

There was a strange smile on his face, no more than an upward curl of his lip, and a curious, wintery expression in his dark eyes as we stood facing each other across the room. Maybe he did have it in him to kill a man. But not unless the man had his back to him.

I turned my back and walked out.

FOUR

ARCHIE ST. GEORGE's idea of where to pass over a package containing twenty-thousand dollars was in front of the fish house next to Toots Shor's on 51st Street. Well . . .

All he said was: "When you've got her stuff bring it to her at the Park East. Send me your bill in the morning." Then he walked away from me and entered Shor's for his dinner. It was 8:30 that night.

I took one cab to 34th and went downstairs to the Long Island Terminal in Penn Station. A little fat guy took the black briefcase, a dime, and gave me a 24-hour check. I came out of Penn Station through the 33rd Street exit and crossed the street to the dingy-looking, neon-signed Hotel Barnet. I handed the air mail envelope to the clerk and asked for the one he had for me.

St. George had been right. It held the key to a locker. But it wasn't a locker in Grand Central or LaGuardia. It was in the Flatbush Avenue terminal in Brooklyn. Across the river and into the woods.

I took the Seventh Avenue Express and got off at Atlantic Avenue. That platform connects with the terminal and as I went into it and toward the bank of lockers I noticed a curious thing.

Beside the lockers was a row of telephone booths. And though the door was closed on one of them, the light was not on. But it wasn't so dark that I couldn't see the shape of the man sitting inside and gazing out. Seeing him made me sure that the character in brown who had followed me off the subway had also followed me on. And if I turned now he would be putting a penny in the gum machine that faced the lockers.

26

I had a lot to decide and not much time to decide it in. If they were cops—and if the porter sweeping dirt on my left was a third one—then opening that locker was worth the next twenty years of my life. If they were from the mob . . .

A telephone jangled. I looked toward the blacked-out booth. The one inside had turned and was talking into the mouthpiece. Then the door opened and he stepped out and kept walking, very fast, in the opposite direction. I turned in time to see brownie hurrying the same way. The porter kept shovelling dirt onto his dustpan.

The two had been the mob, and the call had just come through from Penn Station that they had their twenty G's. They didn't have to kill me. I opened the locker and took out a medium-heavy box about the right size for a jewelcase wrapped in gray paper.

I carried it under my arm out to Flatbush Avenue and bribed a hackie to take me back to Manhattan. A doorman—no less—ushered me out of the cab and into the hushed, high-ceilinged lobby of the very expensive Park East Hotel.

The woman at the desk called upstairs and then told me to go on up to suite 5 in the penthouse. The elevator was express all the way and I stepped from it and plunged nearly to my ankles in a royal-blue corridor carpet.

I touched the button beside the door numbered '5' and it was opened immediately.

Kyle Shannon stood there, all in white, her red hair pulled back behind her ears and for five beats I didn't breathe.

"Come in," she said brittlely.

I waited until she was safely out of the way and then crossed her threshold. The nearest feeling I'd had to this was a good sixteen years before.

The door closed softly at my back and she led me through a wide foyer into a tremendous living room. It must have been thirty feet long and almost that wide. She stopped and turned.

"May I have it?"

I handed the package to her.

She took it and strode swiftly toward an archway at the far end of the room. She passed through it and I was left alone.

I walked in the direction of the huge window on the left, wishing I could appreciate the thousands of dollars that had gone into decorating the room. All I knew—from the pair of gently curving couches, the comfortable-looking chairs, the eye-resting, wall-to-wall carpet and the velvet drapes that hung from ceiling to floor—was that I liked it. There was a small, leather-topped table that held a lamp and a framed picture. The picture showed a very tall, very handsome white-haired man with what can only be described as a granite jaw. He stood in work clothes, khaki pants and white shirt open at the neck, and his hands rested on the shoulders of a long-legged, exceptionally pretty girl who was eleven or twelve. The picture was black-and-white, but I knew the girl had red hair and that she was Kyle Shannon. The man behind her could be no one else but her father. He certainly looked like somebody who could separate aluminium from rocks. They both wore easy smiles and there was something about the relaxed manner that he held her that explained how good he felt about her.

The window looked directly down on Central Park. The pattern of the roads that cut through it was outlined by street lamps and an occasional convoy of cars passing east and west, north and south. I could make out the lake, strangely enough, because it was a blacker black than the forest of trees around it. I raised my eyes above the park, toward the Hudson River and the necklace of lights that bordered the express highway. A dimly lit ship—it must have been a tanker—glided slowly down the river toward the Narrows, if it was going that far, and the ocean, which lay in a line directly southwest of the spotlighted dome of the Empire State Building.

There were a lot of people, even in my view, doing a

lot of different things. With each other, for each other, to each other. Especially *to*.

"There seems to be something missing." Her voice was close to me, though I hadn't heard her come up, and coldly accusing. More than that, it sounded tired, resigned to some fact of life.

I turned and found her standing with the jewelcase in her hands.

"What is missing?" I asked.

"Why don't we drop the acting?" she said. "You didn't convince me this afternoon and it's getting to be too much to take tonight." Her strong voice wavered.

"What is missing?" I asked her again.

"The *pictures!*" It had been an only half-stifled scream and a crescent of moisture had suddenly appeared below her eyes.

I found myself very close to her, fighting the impulse to take her shoulders in my hands. "*What* pictures? Who the hell said anything about pictures this afternoon?"

She threw her head back. A humorless, unmusical laugh burst from her throat. "What have you got to gain, Mr. Barney Glines?" The tears had drained away as quickly as they'd appeared. Her voice cut into me, sharper than any knife. "You and your filthy friends have me! I'm willing to do *business!*"

I had to hold her then. Had to do something with my hands. That or knock her to the floor.

She spun, writhing, trying to get away from me. I tightened and pulled her close—jammed her to me—and looked down into her fiercely excited face.

"Listen to me! I had nothing to do with your robbery. I don't know anything about your pictures. I *don't know* a goddamn thing!"

I dropped my hands and stepped away from her. We were both breathing hard. When I spoke again my voice was low, under control. "Tell me what's going on," I said to her. "Tell me about these pictures."

She was looking at me curiously. Indecision filled her eyes, clouded her face.

"You—you don't really know?" Her voice was wary, on the fence, ready to fall either way.

"I know that Archie St. George called me this morning," I said. "I came over to his office and heard him tell me about your picture and your robbery last night. It was the first time."

"Then why was I told to get in touch with you if I wanted my jewelcase back?"

"I don't know why," I admitted.

Her eyes were suspicious again.

"What are these pictures?" I asked.

She said nothing.

"Look," I said. "On one side you've got a theft and a phone call tying me into it. Now suppose you'd immediately gotten the police—as you should have. The first person they'd pick up is me. But not for questioning, not the way they'd grab Joe Doakes if you'd been told to contact him. I work *with* the police," I told her, "not against them. I hate to be the one telling you this, but my record in this town is clean. This is the first time," I said, "that I've stepped out of line."

While I'd been speaking she had turned and walked to one of the small couches. Now she was sitting, her beautiful head raised, looking at me across the width of the room.

"Why did you?"

"To find out who was trying to use me," I answered. "To nail them when you had your property back. To . . ." I stopped. Why tell her my other reason for getting into this thing?

"To *what?*"

"Nothing. Now what about these pictures? What is this thing all about?"

She ran her hand across her eyes. Her head shook from side to side. "I don't know what to believe . . . what to do . . ."

I came across the room slowly. "Here," I said, holding a package of cigarettes to her. She took one and I leaned down to light it. Our eyes met and locked for an instant in the flame. Then the match was out.

"That picture over on the table," I said. "That's your father, isn't it?"

She nodded.

"I got the feeling when I looked at it that you two were rather close."

"Yes," she said. "We were. Very, very close."

I had my wallet in my hand. From it I took a dog-eared snapshot and handed it to her. On it was a broad-shouldered grinning man as tall as I am. He had a long arm wrapped around the shoulder of a blond-haired boy of fifteen.

"This is you," she said.

"And the man is my father."

"He's in uniform," she said. "A police uniform." She looked up at me.

"He was a captain," I told her. "Right here in Manhattan. Right in this neighborhood, as a matter of fact. He commanded the 19th Precinct."

"Is he . . . ?"

"He was killed. Four gunmen came into our house one night. My mother was visiting across the street. I was playing in a basketball game. My father opened the door and they killed him with sixteen bullets."

"Oh, *no!* But why . . . ?"

"The 19th Precinct, on its own hook, was cleaning up this section of town. Running the racket boys and the mobsters out of the neighborhood." I watched her. "The four who killed him turned out to be hired by a hijacking crowd. Their business was furs," I said. "Furs and jewelry. Sneak-thieves were one thing my father couldn't abide. Breaking into a man's home, violating his privacy, was his idea of the worst crime on the books."

She stood up. "I see," she said, her voice low. "And I'm sorry."

"Now why don't we trust each other a little and try to find out what's going on?"

"All right. Would you like a drink? I know I could use one."

"Sure. Tell me where it is and I'll make some."

"There's a service pantry in there," she said, pointing to the archway. "The liquor is in that cabinet." She indicated the place.

I went through the arch. At the end of a short hall I found the service pantry—a tiny room with a sink, glasses, cabinet and refrigerator. On the way back I glanced into the bedroom. Its walls were a deep rose and on each side of the bed were end-tables bearing a pair of rose shaded lamps that gave the room a glowing warmth. The chambermaid had turned the covers down below one of the bed's two pillows. On top of a dresser was a picture of Archie St. George. It was a good likeness.

Her choice was scotch and soda. I mixed myself a rye and water and took the drinks to her. She was sitting again on the couch and I picked one of the chairs for myself.

"Well," she began, "to begin with, I didn't want all this secrecy about the robbery because of the movie I made. I suppose it would hurt the fantastic publicity buildup they've got prepared and make the studio look silly—but if all they'd stolen was the jewelry I'd have gone straight to the police. But there was something else in the jewel-case. Some pictures," she said, "stuck away in the bottom."

"What kind of pictures?"

She took a breath. "When I first arrived in New York," she said, "I landed a job as a model. I didn't know a soul and moved into the Barbizon Hotel for women. My room-mate, Gloria Dennis, was a dancer—a showgirl, I'd guess you'd call her. She was also an amateur photographer. Well, after a few months I was finally making a go of it. Then one day a copy of *Vogue* came out and there was a three page layout on me. I was modelling a trousseau

—from panties to mink coat. The photographer was Tony Bouchard, and I guess he's the one who invented the idea of the haughty, statuesque type model. You know—head back, eyes almost completely closed, hands on hips. You're supposed to look completely unapproachable."

She sipped again on her highball. "When I got back to the hotel that night I found that Gloria and some of our pals had plastered the pages of the magazine all over the room. Everywhere I turned, there was this cold fish staring out at me. And the kidding! It went on for hours. I couldn't blame them," she said. "The pictures *were* pretty ridiculous. Then Gloria had an idea. She got one of the other showgirls, Pat something, to take off her clothes and pose just as I had in *Vogue*. It was the most hilarious thing we'd ever seen. It's just impossible," she explained, "to look like the world's most obnoxious snob when you haven't got a thing on your back. But Pat didn't quite bring it off. They all started demanding that the only one who could do it justice was me. I didn't want any part of it. Then they conducted a trial and the jury voted me guilty of betraying the female sex in *Vogue* magazine. The sentence was to pose for the same series, undraped, and let Gloria photograph me. That," she said, "was two years ago. I was all of eighteen and trying to prove to everybody in New York that being W. R. Shannon's daughter hadn't gone to my head. I had to be a good sport, or die trying. So . . ." She looked down into her glass.

"Where are the negatives?" I asked.

"They were in the jewelcase," she said. "Along with the prints. Gloria gave them to me right after they were developed and everybody had a good laugh."

"How did you happen to keep them around?"

She shook her head. "I don't know how many times I started to destroy them. It was . . ." She looked at me and there was a rueful smile across her face.

"Okay. Now the pictures are gone. You paid twenty-thousand dollars for them and didn't get them. When you got that call last night, did he mention the pictures?"

"Not a word. He just said I could have my things back and to contact you."

"Why didn't St. George mention the pictures to me?"

"Archie? He doesn't know anything about them."

I watched her over the edge of my glass. "You didn't tell him?"

She shook her head. "There was no reason to. I only called Archie because— Well, I was scared to death." She flashed me a smile. "I didn't know who or what this Barney Glines was going to turn out to be."

"No, you didn't. You and St. George are a little more than client and agent, aren't you?"

Her eyebrows went up.

"Aren't you?"

"They've got a stock answer for that out in Hollywood," she told me. "Mr. St. George and I are very good friends."

"How long have you known him?"

"Archie, as they say, 'discovered' me. He really did. That story he told you about a producer seeing a stocking ad and giving me a test— It wasn't a producer. It was Archie. That was a year and a half ago."

"Are you going to marry him?"

She laughed. "You certainly are direct. To tell you the truth, I don't know. He's asked me . . ." She shrugged her shoulders. "I just don't know. There's a difference," she said slowly, "between an affair and a marriage. Are you married?"

"No," I said. "I'm not." I got up.

"Wouldn't you like another drink? Archie is coming over later on. A client of his is opening in a show tonight and we're all going to a little party . . ."

I laughed. "That wouldn't include me," I told her. "I almost knocked your boyfriend's nose out of joint this afternoon."

"You *what?*" She came to her feet gracefully. "But why?"

I said it as softly as I could. "Archie St. George is a son of a bitch, Miss Shannon. An all-American son of a bitch."

Her green eyes began to blaze and I turned away from her. "I'll see what I can do about your pictures," I told her over my shoulder.

"Maybe you'd better not bother, Mr. Glines. If you and Archie don't like each other . . ."

"Oh, I want to get them back for myself as much as for you. I have to get a bad smell out of my nose. So long."

I let myself out of the suite. But all the way back to the *Clubhouse Bar*—my after-hours office—I couldn't get that face and the red hair and the white dress out of my mind. That Archie St. George sure could pick 'em.

FIVE

THE *Clubhouse Bar* is off Madison at 39th and there is nothing to distinguish it from any other except the small sign stuck in the window. "No Television," it reads, and that attracted me inside three years ago and has kept me coming back ever since. Peace, it's wonderful. No frustrated ballplayers getting elbow callus from second guessing Durocher. No bleary-eyed experts yelling the wrong answers to the quizmaster. No turning your head to find the guy on the next stool hanging over your shoulder to see down the front of Faye Emerson's dress.

You come to the *Clubhouse* for a drink. It's a place to think in, to relax in. To talk, if that's what you need, to Tommy Parise, the owner and nighttime barkeep.

"What's eating you?" he asked when he saw my face.

I shook my head. Nothing was eating me but the fact that it was night. The people who could get me started after the thieves—the salesmen at the Cadillac agencies, the registration clerks down at Worth Street—were all at home with their feet in slippers. The two night clerks were no good to me. Either they would not talk, period, or I could buy a description of a man neither one had ever seen before but he had a face like a hatchet.

But I could go and talk to them. I could get up right now and go over to the Leewood Hotel. But I didn't. Kyle Shannon kept getting in the way.

Kyle Shannon loves Archie St. George. Well, not quite. She goes for him, but not big. She keeps a picture of him in her bedroom and he seems to have the inside track on her time. But there was no mistaking the hesitancy in her voice, a cloud behind her eyes, when I asked her about him. Something was troubling her about Archie. Something vague, that she couldn't put into words—if she was even aware of it at all.

But how about Archie for Kyle? How big was that? He'd asked her to marry him. That, for Archie, didn't have to mean anything at all. And I couldn't get that secretary of his out of my mind—the one he'd been belting around in his office. That kid hadn't been crying because her face hurt. It was something that went deeper.

And there was Archie's face when he'd warned me away from Kyle. The warning I could understand—but not the words. If a girl, any girl, is a "piece" in your mind, what kind of marriage are you planning?

I left the cab at 57th Street, stood on the corner until it was gone, and then doubled back to 56th. 56th, between Fifth and Sixth Avenues, is a very quiet, very respectable block of art galleries and old brownstones converted into apartments. I stopped before the one where Archie St. George lived and climbed the flight of stone steps to the 'parlor floor.' In the vestibule was a directory of four names. "A. St. George," it turned out, occupied the street level floor. I descended the steps to the street, walked alongside the staircase and stopped before the door of St. George's home.

All right, I thought, all *right*. I can hear you, Pop. You're coming in clear. But I am going inside Archie St. George's home and Archie St. George isn't there. I know he isn't there because I was told he was at the theatre tonight. Yes, just like any lousy fingerman, like the cat-burglars you hated so hard, here I am and I'm going inside. I can hear you, Pop, and I can see the storm lines in your face. But you never met Kyle Shannon.

I went to work on the "burglar-proof" lock and jockeyed it open five minutes later. All that people have to do—but which they never do—is double-lock it with their key from the outside. That throws home a brass bolt that breaks the heart of any pickman.

I moved around in the dark inside, checking the blinds and getting my lungs full of stale cigarette smoke and the very particular odor of warm vermouth. Then I found my way to a lamp and turned it on. I was in an expensive place. This was the living room, done but modern, and featuring a blond maple cocktail table that reached midway up my shinbone and must have been three yards square. There was a couch along one wall that was five cushions wide and had no arms. The next largest piece was thirty feet away, almost at the other end of the room, and it was an armless thing that could have been a bed at half mast or a chair. Scattered haphazardly on the kelly green wall-to-wall rug were other chairs, and the one that caught my eye but not my fancy was a seat that seemed to be made by unbending a giant paper clip.

There was also the inevitable television set, this one a custom job with what must have been 900 square inches of screen. Holding down an important corner was an elaborate bar, complete with one stool, and resting on it was a shaker holding the dregs of martinis and four unwashed cocktail glasses.

This was the house that Archie built, peddling flesh at ten percent. And what, exactly, had I busted in here for? What had I expected to find? The answer was nothing and the answer was everything. Then I had to admit it: I was here because Kyle Shannon liked Archie St. George and I didn't. I was more interested, right now, right here, in throwing a big hook into St. George than in getting back Kyle's pictures.

But what the hell was I looking for? Did I really think that all I had to do was open a drawer and find her pictures?

I left the room I was in and went deeper into the apartment. It had two bedrooms. The small one was decorated neutrally—at first glance—but then a pinkishness came through, and the realization that a woman would be more at home in here than a man. Sure enough, in the middle dresser drawer, and still wrapped in store tissue, were one pair of black lace panties, one brassiere and one negligee. Emergency rations, but how thoughtful.

His bedroom was all male and a smile wide. On the floor were two scatter rugs made to look like bearskins but with the heads thoughtfully omitted. On the wall were lithographs of racehorses and hunting scenes. Two night tables held lamps that were horses' bodies. The bed was two three-quarter beds that had been joined but made up separately.

That, I realized, was one of the things that I'd come here to find out about Archie St. George.

The top drawer of his dresser showed handkerchiefs, a leather case and socks, socks, socks. The case held a wrist watch and studs. I began to juggle the sockrolls, with nothing special in mind, when I came across one with a stiffened back. My fingers pulled out a thin rectangle that was an address book. A little black book, except that this was brown. And it was crammed with the names of women, their addresses and their telephone numbers.

Some of them, as is bound to happen, had either died, moved and left no forwarding address, lost their appeal or gotten married. They were noted by a line drawn through their names. I flipped the pages idly, wondering, maybe, if we had any friends in common. My eye stopped on the name, *Gloria Dennis*. Did I know Gloria Dennis . . . ?

No, but Kyle Shannon did. That was the girl Kyle had roomed with, the showgirl with the trouble-making camera.

And a few pages later, sandwiched between someone named Bea Benedict and someone else named Joan Van-Cott, was *Kyle Shannon*. No stars next to her name, no underline, no exclamation point. Just "Kyle Shannon, Barbizon."

But Kyle had told me she had left the Barbizon two years before, which not only dated Archie's little book

but made the entry curious. I replaced it in the sockroll
and strolled back to the enormous living room. Sticking
out from the magazine rack, next to a copy of *Stag*, was
this week's *Variety*. It had been folded on the 'Showbill'
page—a service for bookers, actors, agents and bill col-
lectors that records towns and places where new acts
have opened. Of the thirty some odd listed, five were
circled in pencil. Archie's clients? Two were singing
combinations, one was a strip act, one a singing solo
and the fifth was a comedian. The only act in Manhattan
was the stripper, who worked under the handicap of
"Gaye Dawn" and had opened last night at *The Jungle*,
a trap I knew vaguely as one of the holes in the wall
along 52nd Street.

I slipped the showpaper back in its place, turned out
the lamp and left the apartment. I headed south to 52nd.

Hell, suppose Archie St. George had seen Kyle Shannon's legs in a hosiery ad? And suppose, ridiculous as it
sounded, he actually had checked back through the
magazine and located the model agency and then the
photographer? Even if I had believed such a story, why
was Gloria Dennis listed in St. George's book *before*
Kyle Shannon? If he knew Gloria Dennis why wouldn't
he have heard about her roommate? Why all the junk
about "discovering" her?

But what really intrigued me was the coincidence of
initials in Gloria Dennis and Gaye Dawn, the strip-
teaser.

The Jungle, from the front door to the fire exit that
probably wouldn't open, couldn't have been thirty feet
long. And from the tiny bar on one side to the hatcheck
booth on the other, it was not more than five short
strides. I took only two of them though, when I stopped
short. Whatever my plans were, they needed changing,
for the hatchet-faced lad of the Leewood Hotel was sitting at the end of the bar facing the small bandstand and
the tables ringing the tiny dance floor.

I edged back toward the hatcheck and made my way to the dozen small tables, keeping myself close to the dark wall and my face averted. I sat down at one that gave me a clear look at the bar, and before a waiter arrived there was a chord from the four-piece band, the houselights went out completely and a powerful, multicolored spot shone down on a small circle of the floor.

There was no master of ceremonies, no welcome, no dirty jokes. Just a voice on a public address system.

"From Hollywood, ladies and gentlemen," it said to the less than thirty of us present, "the exotic, erotic Gaye Dawn!"

Another brassy blast from the band, a curtain parted, and onto the floor came a tall, leggy, sultry-mouthed brunette. Exotic, no. But erotic, definitely. One half of her body was clothed in a black dress slit to the thigh. The other half was in one leg of men's trousers and part of a shirt that was open at the neck and sewn to the neckline of the dress. On the female half of her face the black hair hung below her shoulders; on the other it was cut short and brushed manstyle to her scalp. Only one side of her mouth carried lipstick.

She came to the center of the floor, stopped for a moment and then—so help me God—wrapped the "man's" arm around her waist and began revolving slowly. The tempo picked up. She spun more quickly and the illusion of two people dancing was very real—helped no little by the crazily turning spotlights.

Then—with a bang—the spinning ended and the male half was bent over the female. Its hand begun to explore but was resisted by the female hand—her own fingers wrapped tightly around her own wrist, if you're still with me. But the held hand would not be put off. Its fingers forced the wrist down slowly. A sudden lunge and the front of the gown was ripped away.

Gaye Dawn should have straightened up then, bowed and disappeared. Her act had a good gimmick and she seemed to have some talent for drama. But art is art and this was *The Jungle*, 52nd Street, New York 19, N.Y.

The music stopped being music at that point and became a series of staccato drumshots as the "man" began taking the "woman's" dress off. Now it was pornography, down around the geek level.

Then the lights went off and there was applause. A moment later the lights came up. Gaye Dawn was gone and two kids with their hair dyed platinum came onto the floor. "Ladies and gentlemen," droned the public address, "presenting the Lamour twins, Laverne and Labelle, and their sensational double-strip . . ."

I watched my man at the bar slip from his stool and make his way around the tables across the room toward the curtain that led backstage. For the second time tonight I paid for a drink I hadn't tasted and got up to follow.

Beyond the curtain was a narrow hallway. Four doors, all closed, led off it, and at the far end was the fire exit. A card stuck in a holder on the door at my right read "Gaye Dawn," and from inside came the voice of an angry girl.

". . . you three seconds to get out of here, Frankie, before I call Mr. Solomon!"

That made Frankie laugh. But when he spoke he wasn't happy. "You were told to stay out of town," he said. "What the hell's the idea coming back? Who booked you into this joint?"

"I booked myself in! Now get out!"

"What's the matter, baby? You late for a shot?"

Her voice went up dangerously. "Leave me alone! Get out!"

I heard his feet cross the room swiftly. "Where do you hide it, baby?" he asked viciously. "Here?" There was a sound a trunk would make if it were scraped across wood. A lid was thrown back.

"No! No! Don't take it, Frankie! Don't!"

There was a sharp blow—a hand against a cheek. The girl screamed and I went into the room.

She was on the floor, wearing part of the costume, holding her hand to her cheek. A childish whimper came from her throat and her eyes were upturned to Frankie's face, pleadingly.

He whirled to face me. For an instant he didn't recognize me. But only for an instant. In his left hand he held a small silver box. In the other was an all-glass syringe, the needle already in place.

The box disappeared into his overcoat pocket. The hand came back holding a palm-sized .32.

"Keep coming," he told me softly. "Leave the door open." A wave of the gun hand motioned me to move to the wall. I moved.

He crossed the room and turned, his back in the open doorway. "Catch the next train west," he told the girl. His eyes raised to mine. "You're in trouble, hero," he said. "You're in a jam."

Then his hand was on the doorknob, pulling it after him, and he was gone. The closing door seemed to bring Gaye Dawn to life. She scrambled up from the floor, shouting hysterically, and would have followed him if I hadn't held her.

"Let go, let go! *Let-me-alone!*" She tried to pull loose by squirming away from me.

"Easy," I told her, knowing it would do no good. Her face was drawn and there was an animal wildness in her eyes. "You can't catch him now. He's gone."

"No." she cried, shaking her head fitfully. "He can't go. He's got the . . ." She looked up at me and stopped speaking. Suddenly her face contorted in rage and she just missed raking my cheeks with her fingernails. "Who are you?" she screamed. "It's your fault. Let me go!"

I clamped my hand over her mouth, taking the chance of getting bitten in order to quiet her down long enough to tell her something. I pulled her face close to my mouth and spoke as earnestly as I could.

"I can get you a fix," I said. "Do you hear?" She still

fought like a cat to get away. "A joyride," I promised her. "From here to Vinegarville. You hear?"

She was quieter. Her eyes stared straight up into my own, like two prayers.

"It's on the level," I assured her. I looked around. "But I can't get it delivered here." I dropped my hand from her mouth. "Where can we go?"

"My place," she said and stepped past me quickly. I turned to find her stepping out of the shambles of her costume. The G-string followed it in a heap on the floor. She went to a curtained closet, pulled a gray dress from it and quickly pulled it over her body. She began buttoning up the back feverishly. Her fingers couldn't make it.

"Easy," I told her again and stepped over to help. "Where's your coat?"

She pointed to the closet and while I was taking down a full length beaver fur she stepped to her dressing table, unloosened the hair on the "man" side, drew lipstick over both halves of her lips and turned to me. I got her into the coat and we left *The Jungle* without speaking.

The cab took us crosstown, past 8th, past 9th, then south for half a dozen blocks into Hell's Kitchen. It stopped in front of a drab, three-story building that looked like every other drab, three-story building on either side of the block. I paid the hackie while she scooted out of the cab and up the short flight of steps to the house. When I got into the vestibule she was already halfway to the second floor.

"Wait," I said. "Do you have a phone?" It was the first thing we'd said to each other in fifteen minutes.

She nodded her head and I followed her up the creaking steps and into a room halfway down the dreary hall.

Inside was a bed, unmade. On a wooden chair was a piece of luggage, open, showing some folded dresses. On the chipped bureau was a half-emptied quart of rye and beside it a heavy-bottomed bathroom glass.

I found her pointing at the telephone. The hand at the end of her arm trembled violently. I went to it and dialed. To the man who answered, I said: "I want Andy Aliberto. Barney Glines is calling him."

Andy came on in seconds.

"I can't talk too long, Andy. I got over on your side of the street by accident. It may wind up in something you're after."

"What is it?"

"Somebody who might be pushing the 52nd Street beat. I'm with somebody now who could turn the key."

"Is he in bad shape?"

"She," I answered. "Bad enough. I need a deck of heroin, from the looks of her. And the fixings."

"Where are you?"

I gave him the address.

"Will do, Barney. And thanks for sticking your neck out for the Narcotics Bureau."

Then the agent and I hung up and I turned to Gaye Dawn. She was lying on the bed, the coat still on, her arms rigidly at her side.

"It'll be along soon," I said but the way she kept staring at the ceiling iced my heart. This was the calm before the God-awful storm. A wing-ding was coming and all I could do was pray Aliberto would make the long trip from his office on 90 Church before it arrived.

But this wasn't to be my lucky night. I had my back to her, standing at the window and looking through the crack in the shade, when she screamed.

I didn't want to turn around. I had to. The sound that came from her throat was a claw ripping my stomach. She was writhing on the bed, her head twisting one way, her body going the other. Her legs jerked in grotesque spasms—a puppet dancing and a madman held the strings.

Then one convulsion turned her completely on her stomach, and with the same movement her arms shot out and pushed her rigidly to her knees. She held that position, staring down at the bed, and from her parted lips came the unearthly wail of nerves tormented to within a slim shadow of insanity.

I got there and threw my arms around her, trying to pin her to the bed. She couldn't have weighed 125 pounds. Her body heaved and my 180 might have been that many feathers. The suddenness broke my hold and the momentum carried us both from the bed to the floor.

"Fix me! *Fix* me!" It was a wild screech, a sound from some private hell.

I reached out for her again, to keep her off her feet, to keep her from plunging through the window. Anything.

She pushed against me and her body gave a tremendous, arching jerk backward. Two men couldn't have held her. She rose to her knees and threw the fur coat from her shoulders. She climbed to her feet. Her hand dug into the neck of her dress and ripped it from her body as though it were tissue paper. She spun and my fingers wrapped around an ankle, raised in full flight toward the window, and she came down on the rug with a thud that would have stunned anyone but an addict overdue for a shot.

But all she did was coil into a knot, naked knees jammed against breasts, and then launch herself on top of me. I got a glimpse of fingers bent like claws. I threw my own hands up, inside her elbows, but not soon enough to keep her from shredding the side of my face with her nails.

And then she went lax. A dead weight across my body, loose as a rag doll. I eased her gently to the floor, knowing what the hell *this* was. Act one curtain. Act two coming up. They have been known—the male junkies—to tear holes in straitjackets during the second attack. But now there wasn't a sound from her, not a murmur.

Someone knocked softly on the door. I watched her as I climbed to my feet. She was lying on her back, arms and legs spread wide, her eyes staring unseeingly at the

ceiling and her tongue clamped between two rows of
tiny white teeth. I prayed she wouldn't bite it in two
before I got back from the door.

"Andy?" I asked, and found my voice shaking badly.

"Andy," he answered.

I opened the door a crack.

"Give," I said.

He handed a small, paper-wrapped package to me.
"You all right in here?"

"I'm fine," I lied.

"You want some help, Barney?"

I shook my head.

"Don't get fooled by the women," he said. "They're
worse than the men."

I nodded my head. "I better set this up," I told him.

"Sure. Don't forget to write it all down, will you,
Barney?"

"You'll get a report in the morning, Andy."

"Swell, Barney. Good luck." His face was gone then
and I closed the door.

She hadn't moved a muscle. Her teeth still clamped
down on her tongue. But there was a sound deep in her
chest, a soft moaning. I opened the package from the Narcotics Bureau and got busy fast. Fast but carefully. The
heroin, I knew, would be pure and uncut—as fine a derivative as a respectable drug firm could supply. The dis-
solvent would be the clearest glucose obtainable. And the
needle would be sterile. Gloria Dennis, alias Gaye Dawn,
God save her, never would have it this good again.

I lifted her in my arms and carried her to the bed. She
was as limp and pliable as 125 pounds of flour. I turned
her forearm around. Beneath some sort of makeup paint
she used I made out half a dozen pinpricks, some healing,
some very fresh. I found a blue vein, burst through the
skin and closed the syringe slowly and steadily.

Then I got up and walked to the window again. How
many years ago had I stood here, looking past the shade
into the dark, dirty, peaceful street below?

Sixty seconds went by. I lit a cigarette. As I laid the match on the windowsill she spoke to me.

"Come here," she said. It was a nice voice once. Now it was still warm, but it was tired with a weariness all the narcotics in the world couldn't relieve.

I turned around. She was still on her back, still naked, but now her body was draped like a woman's. Not like before. I went over.

"Cigarette?"

Her head moved from side to side on the pillow. She smiled lazily at me. "All I need is you, darling. The big, beautiful man who fixed me so good ..." Right in the middle of a word she yawned and stretched luxuriously. "Got a kiss for me, baby-boy?"

I shut my eyes for a moment. Things weren't bad enough—I had to humor a nymphomaniac. Maybe that was how she'd gotten on the junk in the beginning. You could let go with a little hemp-joy in your blood. And your head was clear as a bell, every second. Every big, beautiful, baby-this-is-living-second.

Then one night something went wrong. You and this guy are lying there on this bed—who remembers his name? who cares where the bed was?—and you're both smoking and waiting. And waiting. You hold the reefer until the ash singes your fingers. But nothing happens. You're still tense and restless. If he turns toward you, if he so much as touches you with his dirty hand—whoever he is—you'll scream. You get another cigarette going. He doesn't like it. He says something nasty and does something with his hand you can't stand. Can't stand because you're not loose. Can't he understand, the filthy son of a bitch! Whatever happens after you kick at him and hit him and yell you'd just as soon forget.

A week later you try again. New guy, new bed. The cigarettes are no good, no good at all! But this guy is a smoothie. He tells you not to blame the reefer. You're a big girl now, he says. Marijuana's for the babies. For little kids who don't know what living really is. The thing for

you is the Horse. A little sniff of Horse, that's all, beautiful. Then you and me are gonna ride ...

And he just happens to have a little happy powder with
him. Or he knows where he can get it, for free. It turns
out he's right. You *are* a big girl now, and this *is* living.
But it's not free. Only the sample was free, only the first
ride. Then it costs. And funny thing, you get to need it
for a lot more than letting your libido out of its cage.
You need it at least once a day. Sometime late in the
afternoon. That's when you get restless, when the gnaw-
ing begins. Then you need it earlier in the day, too. Pretty
soon you have to have it within an hour after you wake
up. Then you find out the facts of life: The more you
need to get fixed, the more expensive it gets. And oh,
how you need to get fixed!

I opened my eyes and looked into hers.

"Come on," she was saying. "Don't keep a lady waiting ..."

You can't keep them waiting. Their selfishness, their
self-love, lets nothing stand in the way. It's a fire, con-
suming them and everyone they touch. It gives nothing,
takes everything.

"Listen, Gloria," I started to say and that was as far as
I got.

"Name's Gaye," she drawled, yawning again. "Strip,
man. Get free ..." Her eyes lost some of their bottom-
less depth. They almost focused. "How'd you know about
Gloria? Who are you, man?" She giggled and touched me
with her hand. Like a child, like a bad little girl.

I held her wrist and she giggled again.

"Kyle Shannon told me all about you, Gloria," I said
and waited. You do a lot of waiting with mainliners. Your
world and their world move at different speeds. Andy
Aliberto is the source for this: One of his informers (the
Narcotics Bureau pays them off in heroin, which is a
thousand times more valuable than money) slipped him
into a party in East Harlem one night. When everybody
was happy, one of the girls said, "I feel real, real good."

None of the other seven people in the room said anything. Five minutes went by in complete silence. Ten minutes. Then, "Me too," answered her boyfriend.

The seconds ticked off while Gloria Dennis and I looked at each other. Then she said, "I sure fixed Kyle good, didn't I?" Another giggle. "Not like you fixed me, darling. Come on . . ."

"They must have been good pictures," I said. "Who did you talk to about them?"

I gave my voice a quicker tempo, knowing it wouldn't do any good. It didn't. She let an agonizing minute go by.

"Come on," she said again. "I don't want to talk now. Come on . . ."

She didn't want to talk now. Would she want to talk later? Or what was next on the program? I stared down at her and I knew she could throw the door wide open. Kyle Shannon's troubles began the day she met Gloria Dennis. And Gloria Dennis' troubles began the day she met . . .

"Are you or aren't you?" Her voice was quicker now, meaner. The mew of a cat to the snarl of a cat. "God, don't tell me the big strong man is queer . . ." Another yawn.

The last thing I wanted to do was service Gloria Dennis. But I wanted her story. I had just begun taking my jacket from my shoulders when the door quietly opened and two men slipped swiftly into the room.

One was Frankie. The other I was seeing for the first time and not liking what I saw in his face. Both were armed, but Frankie had changed his toy for a mansized .38, which he held confidently in his gloved right hand.

No one spoke a word. The stranger held his gun tilted upward toward the center of my face. Frankie swung his toward the girl in the bed, planted his feet solidly, and fired five times into her body. As they still echoed, even before the powder odor formed, he had dropped the .38 to the floor and was on his way out of the room, his friend backing behind him. The door was quietly closed.

Still no one spoke. The naked corpse on the bed grinned idiotically, as though having said something smart and waiting for a reaction. One of the slugs had entered her head, or two of them, and as I watched, the black hair became moist and dark brown in one small spot. She began to bleed along the side of her breast, and at her ribs, and I turned away and went to the telephone.

I called the 16th Precinct. The cop said she might not be dead and he'd get the ambulance. I think that he thought I was drunk and my trouble was domestic. I called Homicide West. Harry Larkin was on sick leave but the intelligent-sounding duty officer would send a squad right up. He added, for free, that he didn't know me but had heard the name.

The receiver was on its cradle two minutes when a 16th Precinct patrol car jammed to a stop on the street and two blue-overcoated cops stepped from it and came up the street steps. I heard their feet on the stairway and held the door ajar when they turned the corner. They both held tight to their revolvers but relief was plain on their faces. Answering trouble calls in Hell's Kitchen after dark is worth a hell of a lot more than $55 a week.

"You won't like what you see," I warned them, but before they got to me two doors opened on the hallway.

A short, heavy-set woman stepped out of one of them.

"I heard it all," she announced. "The girl was screaming her head off. Then it got quiet. Then the shots." The words tumbled from her lips like potatoes through a hole. She darted a look at me. "That one!" she bellowed. "I saw them come in, him and the girl. *Him!*"

Both cops squared away, their .38's levelled at my stomach.

From the other doorway came a man's voice. He stayed inside his room. "What the hell's going on?" he asked querulously. "Who's making all the goddamned racket?" The cops came toward me slowly, their faces tense. I held out my empty hands and even came out of the room to meet them.

"A woman was killed in here," I said to the older one. "Two guys just opened the door and let fly."

"Turn around," the older one commanded. "Face the wall and put your hands against it."

I did what I was told.

He ran one hand along my body from armpit to ankle. Then the other side.

"All right," he said. "Walk in there. Keep your hands in plain sight."

I led them inside the room.

"Oh, *God*," the cop said, and he said it all. The disgust for death.

I turned around slowly and we looked at each other. I shook my head.

"Then who did?"

"There were two. The trigger man is named Frankie. Five-ten, skinny, Broadway dresser. The other put a gun on me. Same type of punk except shorter and thick. They..."

"Where'd you get this, buddy?" the younger cop interrupted. He was standing by the dresser, looking down at the syringe and the heroin.

I didn't say anything. I watched him leave the dresser and cross to the corpse. He bent down and looked at its upturned forearm.

"You son of a bitch," he said to me, and if I was what he thought I was I'd have agreed with him.

As it was I just kept my mouth shut. The business of the heroin would be handled between two men, one at 90 Church, the other at 240 Centre. Anything Barney Glines said to two harness bulls from the 16th Precinct could complicate it beyond repair.

"She gave you a good fight," the older one told me quietly. I found him staring at the side of my face, at what must have been a raw gash from her nails. I also found him holding Frankie's discarded .38, his finger hooked around the trigger guard.

I still didn't want to talk about anything. Not with them. And I didn't like the way they were making it look.

"Where'd you get this?" he asked me, moving the .38.

"It isn't mine," I said at last, glad to be saying something. "Why don't we just wait a few minutes?"

"Wait for what?"

"The sleuths," I said. "Homicide West is on its way up here . . ."

"Homicide?" He didn't like that. Not at all. For the last few minutes his mind had outraced itself. He saw the front page of *The News,* him and me, the young one in the background and the headline about the mad-dog killer he'd captured after a fight. He saw himself in the Commissioner's office, shaking hands with The Man, getting the commendation ribbon that made him a sergeant for sure. No more riding that goddamned heap eight hours. No more hearing that crackling voice through the speaker sending him to God-knows-what new misery. Or injury. Or death. Now he'd be toasting *his* backside in the station house. Now, thanks to this dope-pushing killer—me —he'd be the voice crackling over some other poor bastard's radio.

I felt sorry for him. But the glamour boys were coming and he'd finished tonight's tour in the patrol car as the same nonentity he'd begun it.

"Who called homicide?" he asked belligerently.

"My name is Glines," I said, beginning an explanation. "I'm a private detective . . ."

"You're a lousy bastard," the young one told me. What was *he* bucking for? third grade detective? Whatever it was, both of them liked me better as a dope pusher who fought with one of his clients and killed her than they did as Glines, with a photostat of his license in his wallet. Which they showed no interest in seeing.

We all heard a car brake to the curb. The young cop crossed quickly to the window and pulled the shade

away. If it had been my mob he'd have been the deadest
cop in New York.

"It's four guys," he told his partner. "Plainclothes," he
added uncertainly.

"The car got an 'N' license?"

He looked and nodded.

"That's them," the older one said dismally. He looked
pathetic, standing there with his shoulders sagging and
his pistol hanging limply at his side. I had the ridiculous
wish that I could be somebody else right now—the guy
they wanted. I wished I were Frankie.

A head appeared at the door. Its face was creased in
a dozen different places and its eyes were hard and wary.
They fanned me and the two men in uniform, pausing
at the drawn pistols, and then a body followed it. Followed by three other men who all turned professionally
to what was on the bed.

One of the newcomers, a compact, mild-faced man
whom I had met before as Lieutenant Stern looked at me.

"Glines, isn't it?" he asked.

I nodded and he made a perfunctory remark about it
being nice to see me again. Then his voice went all
business.

"Who is this?" he asked, indicating Gloria.

I told him, and repeated the facts about 'Frankie' and
his friend. The man from Homicide kept nodding politely.

But then: "Were you making a business call, Glines,
or . . . ?" He let his eyes finish the question discreetly.

I took a deep breath. "I was working," I said, and out
of the corner of my eye I watched two of Stern's detectives examining Gloria's forearm while the young cop
whispered busily.

"I don't mean to crowd you," Stern was saying quietly,
"but what exactly were you working on?"

"The girl was a hophead," I told him. "She had information I could use and possibly some that the Narcotics Bureau could use." Now all six policemen were
staring at me. "I had just given her a shot," I said.

"You?"

I nodded.

"With her stuff?" Stern asked.

I shook my head.

"I see," he said and his shoulders seemed to square. "Where did you get the dope?"

"Come out in the hall, Lieutenant, and I'll tell you."

He stepped forward, but so did two others, including the harness cop. I followed Stern out of the door, and without being too obvious he maneuvered me with my back to the dead end. A detective stood in the doorway, his hand in his coat pocket.

Then, keeping my voice for Stern's ears alone, I told him of Andy Aliberto and the delivery of the heroin from the Bureau.

"I'll have to check you out on all that," he said when I had finished. "But so far as I know you've got a clean bill of health downtown. I'm going to send you home in your own custody, Glines. Just leave your address and telephone number with one of the boys."

I thanked him and he grinned at me. "I've heard a little about your father, too," he said, and his hand rested on my arm for a brief moment.

Then he turned back into the room, forgetting all about me, and I gave the detective at the door the information he needed and left.

It was midnight when I got into bed and 3 A.M. when the ringing of my doorbell wakened me. I opened it to find two of the Homicide detectives standing in the hall. They both came forward without a word, easing me back into the room without actually pushing. One closed the door and stood with his back to it. In his fingers was a .32. The other came on into the room and got between me and the window. He also held a .32 for me to see.

"Get dressed," this one said. "You're arrested."

"For what?"

"For killing Gloria Dennis," he said flatly. "You got any other guns here?"

"Other guns?" My eyes went automatically to my dresser.

"Besides the one you shot her with tonight," he said, walking directly to the dresser and opening drawers.

"That wasn't my gun," I said.

He turned from his search. "No? Then how come it's the .38 registered to you at Centre Street?"

I moved a little stiffly toward the dresser.

"Easy," warned the voice at the door.

I stopped. "My .38 is in the right top drawer," I said. "In the far corner."

I watched him look into the drawer and move his hand all through it.

"Your .38 is down at West 20th Street," he told me, closing the drawer. "And that's where you're going. Get dressed."

I did. As fast as I could. If 'Frankie' and his friends had it in their minds to frame me, they had made a hell of a good start.

SIX

STERN LOOKED at me from behind his desk with disappointment on his face and something that was almost pity in his eyes.

"You can sit down if you want to, Glines," he said softly.

"No thanks," I said and I knew he'd just as soon have me stand. "What's this about my gun?"

"You tell me," he said and waited.

"There's nothing to tell. I didn't have it when I went to the girl's room," I said, "and I sure as hell didn't leave it there."

"Who did?"

"The one who came in and killed her. The one named Frankie. I told you all about it."

"You did. And I've talked to Church Street. It's a little puzzling," he said, looking at me quizzically.

"What is?"

"One half— No, one *part* of your story checks out. You did arrange for an official supply of heroin. You did call here and the local station at what seems to have been right after the shooting."

"And I did wait for the patrol car," I finished, "and everything was just as it had been when they got there."

"That's what bothers me. You do all that after you've just killed a girl," he told me, his voice so quiet I had to bend forward to hear it.

"I killed no one . . ."

He slipped a hand inside a manila envelope on his desk and brought a .38 from it. This he shoved toward me.

"Is this your revolver?"

I looked at it.

"Go ahead, pick it up. Heft it."

I did but I didn't have to. It was mine all right, but in Gloria Dennis' room it had been Frankie's—in his hand and on the floor.

"It's mine," I admitted. "But I didn't use it on that girl."

"Frankie did," Stern told me.

I leaned over his desk. "Yes. *Frankie* did."

"How did Frankie happen to have it?" His voice said 'Frankie' as it would have said 'Uncle Remus.'

"He took it from my room," I said.

"I see. This Frankie has some other name, doesn't he? Or haven't you thought one up for him?"

"Okay, Lieutenant. Book me."

"I'll decide when to book you," he said, his tone thinner than before.

"But I'm through talking about Frankie," I told him.

"Oh?"

"You're working on a homicide," I explained. "I'm not. I say the girl was killed by someone and you say it was me. I say there's a man named Frankie and that he used a gun that turns out to be mine. I say he took it from my room. You don't believe there is a Frankie and you won't believe anything else I have to say about him. So I'm through talking to you."

"Yes," he said. Then, "You say you're not working on a homicide. What are you working on?"

"That's reason number two I'm shutting up. It's my own private business and my client wants it to stay that way."

"Ah," he said, "enter the client. The same old bushmill. What's your client's name?"

I shook my head.

"What's your client's business?"

"No soap," I said. "I'm all through telling about it."

"You think so? Well I say you haven't even started. I want to know why you were in that girl's room. I want to know if she mauled your face while you were raping

her. I want to know if that's when you killed her and got
the half-assed brainstorm that you could feed me to my
ears with the story about Frankie. And don't give me
that crap about getting a lead on some dope drop.
Where's the profit for you? You don't pay your rent with
citations from the Treasury Department. All right, Glines!
Let's have some answers!"

He was good. So good that I was damn glad I hadn't
killed Gloria Dennis.

"I want to know what happened tonight," he insisted.

I shook my head.

He got to his feet quickly. "Okay. Tomorrow's another day. We'll see how you like the Tombs. Bradley!"
he called and the door opened immediately. "Book this
bird on suspicion of homicide and take him to the
Tombs." He turned to me. "Be sure you get good pictures
of those fingernail marks on his face."

I walked out the door without saying anything else.
But Stern's voice struck me in the back. "It's a shame we
can't write you in as John Doe," he said. "Your father's
old friends in the Department are going to be sick when
they read about it in the morning."

And they would hear about it.

Bradley and two uniformed cops had to shoulder their
way through more than a dozen newspaper reporters and
photographers to get me to the desk. Their bulbs popped
in my eyes and their questions dinned in my ears.

"Wouldn't she come across, buddy?"

"You sorry you did it?"

"Who's your lawyer?"

"Was she cheatin' on yuh?"

Then I was looking across the desk at an old, bald-
headed Sergeant and each time I answered him he wrote
it all down in the big black ledger.

Bradley got me out of there and into the Homicide
sedan. We sat in the back with the two cops up front. Several blocks passed in silence.

"Why'd you want to do a thing like that for?" the detective asked me.

"I don't hear a word you say," I told him.

He sighed. "Who you going to get for a lawyer?"

"I don't need a lawyer."

He laughed quietly. "You will when you see the one the City sends down in the morning. Ever talked to one of the D.A.'s little sharpshooters?"

"All the time," I lied.

"You want to stop along the way and pick up anything?" Bradley asked. "Cigarettes? Coffee?"

I shook my head. "I'd like to make a phone call, though."

"We can do that at the Tombs. A lawyer?"

"No. Fellow name of Fred Weaver."

He looked at me. "I know a Fred Weaver that works for Robbery Detail," he said questioningly.

"That's the one."

"Friend of yours?"

"Sometimes," I said.

We arrived and I signed three forms before they let me make my call. Then I was taken to a high-ceilinged cell and the door was locked at my back. I was all alone.

And so was Gloria Dennis.

SEVEN

AT EIGHT O'CLOCK the next morning I found
Fred Weaver, a first grade detective, eyeing me sourly
through the bars of my cell.

"Come on in, Fred," I said, trying to sound as cheer-
fully natural as I could. The key was turned in the lock,
Fred entered, and the big door was re-locked.

I held out my hand and he touched it for a moment
with reluctance. Weaver was pretty much of a cold fish
on any particular day and his lack of enthusiasm now
didn't have to mean anything.

"Thanks for coming down," I told him. He grunted an
answer and avoided my eyes. I pulled the simple metal
chair toward him. He lowered his long bony frame into
it and eased his fedora back on his forehead.

"I need your help, Fred," I began. He looked at me
then but said nothing. "I guess you know what I'm supposed to be in here for."

He nodded glumly.

"But it didn't happen that way, Fred," I said.

He sighed and pulled at his needle-thin nose.

"The hell with whose gun she was shot with," I said.
"The hell with the hypodermic and how my face looks.
Forget them . . ."

He coughed politely into his hand.

"Fred." I had to speak his name to get him to look at
me. "I didn't shoot her, Fred. I didn't make a pass at her.
The girl was a hopeless snowbird. I was up in that room
with her and she was very late for a fix. Not only late
but all worked up to begin with. She'd just finished a
strip act that must have drained her dry. On top of that

61

she had her heroin stolen from her. Can you understand the shape the poor kid was in when I was with her?"

He watched me out of half-closed eyes, his face stiffly uninterested.

"Sure I gave her a shot," I argued. "There isn't a hospital in the city that wouldn't have done the same. All right," I said to the question that flickered in his eyes. "I didn't take her to a hospital. I took her to her room because I thought she could give me some answers I needed. For God's sake, Fred! Do you think I had any idea she was set up to be hit . . . ?"

This wasn't doing me any good. All Fred Weaver knew was what he'd read and heard. I'd killed the girl, period. Why waste his time?

"I was working last night," I started again. "A shakedown." As I spoke I walked around him until the back of his head was facing me. My voice was conversational.

"Shakedown with these lads is a sideline, Fred. Their main business is heisting." The detective's head moved an inch. "Hotel stuff," I added casually. "Jewels, furs, personal letters . . ." He had turned and was looking at me. "A two way operation," I told him. "With a fingerman who knows just what they should look for and when."

"Says who?"

It was nice to hear him speak, even in that tone of voice.

"What do you have about a theft at the Park East Hotel night before last?"

His brow creased for an instant. "There was no theft," he said with authority.

"There was one hundred thousand dollars' worth," I said with as much or more.

He was on his long legs.

"What're you trying to tell me, Barney?"

"Something you won't like. There's a girl," I said. "Knowing her name won't make any difference to you. She was out of her room for a few hours and when she got back she was missing a boxful of jewelry. Then the thieves called her. They arranged ransom and told her to get me to pick them up."

"You?"

"I don't know why, either. But I do know why I went through with it," I said, looking him full in the eyes. "Anyhow, she got her property back. Except for some pictures. That's where the shakedown comes in and that's why I'm still working."

"You did wrong, Barney," Fred Weaver told me.

I nodded agreement.

"I'm marking you lousy in my book," he added.

"There's nothing I can do about that," I said. "But I'm still going to ask you for help."

"You can ask," he said laconically.

"I got a good look at one of the thieves," I said. "He was sitting in the lobby of the Leewood Hotel, spotting me for them. I saw him again inside a place on 52nd Street named *The Jungle*. I saw him again in the girl's room when he killed her with my gun."

Weaver seemed to be trying to rub the skin off his gaunt face with the flat of his palm.

"He's a thin guy," I said. "Built something like you but three or four inches shorter. Got a face you'd like to work on just for the hell of it. His name is Frankie."

After a moment the detective shook his head. "I don't make him," he said.

"I also think he's another junkie. The way he gave it to that girl last night could have come from a needle."

"I still never heard of him."

"Will you go out and look for him for me?"

"Why should I?" he said.

"Because you're a friend of mine," I told him.

Fred Weaver let out a breath. "I guess that's a reason," he said, and a gloomy smile came and went on his pale lips. "You got any ideas where to start looking?"

"I've got one idea," I said and spent the next ten minutes explaining it. He got himself let out of the cell then with the promise he'd do all he could. But I could see he was far from convinced.

The breakfast I had sent out for arrived, along with the newspapers. One of them had a good time on the front page:

POLICE HOLD PRIVATE
EYE FOR STRIP TEASE
DOPE SLAYING

The three column picture on the left below the headline was me standing at the desk next to Bradley. The two column cut on the right was Gloria Dennis undressed as Gaye Dawn. The caption beneath mine spoke of a "love nest," an "orgy" of sex, liquor and heroin and the fact that the "murder weapon" belonged to me. Gloria was described, pretty accurately, as "a beautiful, raven-haired showgirl" and they also used the term "exotic" for her dancing. They gave her age—and I winced—at 21. Inside the newspaper they merely elaborated on the headline and gave fairly complete biographies of both of us. I was naturally referred to as the son of a cop—and was surprised to find that the man who was writing the story was puzzled by what he called "my reputation as a quiet, hardworking, honest investigator" and my serious involvement with "a crime that reeks of sex and vice."

Then my eye was drawn to a seven line box set into the body of the main story. It said that "a chief claims investigator for a leading insurance company, who refused use of his name, told a reporter that despite evidence produced by the police it would require a signed confession by Glines to convince him that the private detective had committed such a crime." That could only be Bruno Holm of Fidelity—and it gave me a strange feeling in my chest.

The turnkey was at the door.

"You want to see a lady name of Miss Shannon?" he asked me.

I got up slowly. "I don't want to see her in here," I answered.

He opened the door. "Come on, then. You can have fifteen minutes with her in the visiting room." I walked at his side down the ancient block, through a main doorway and into a large room that contained a dozen small tables and two chairs at each one.

Kyle Shannon stood to one side, watching me but making no move to come forward. The guard indicated one of the tables—they were all unoccupied—and as he took me to it she walked in the same direction.

She wore a beaver coat, opened to reveal a blue suit beneath it. Perched atop her blonde hair was a blue skullcap.

She had already taken a seat at the table when I arrived. "Fifteen minutes," the guard repeated. "And no nonsense." He walked out of earshot and stood watching the room in general with arms folded across his chest.

We sat watching each other across that little table for almost a minute, neither of us speaking. I don't think I could have, and I was sadly aware of what I must look like, unshaven, mauled, weary-eyed. But even with a bath, a week's sleep and a two hundred-dollar suit I would have been far from fluid seeing her as she looked that morning.

Her first words came as a large shock.

"Did you have to kill Gloria?" she asked.

"No," I said wearily. "I didn't have to kill her. I didn't have to do anything. Anything at all."

I saw then how overwrought she was. "Why do you do it like this?" she asked, her voice rising dangerously. "I was willing from the very start to pay you for my pictures. Why did you . . ."

"What?"

"Oh, don't!" Her eyes moistened. "Wasn't the lie you told me yesterday enough? What have you got to gain any more by pretending innocence? How can it make any difference what *I* think about you?"

"Stop it," I told her. My hand tightened over her wrist. "I didn't kill that girl. Understand? I've never seen your pictures, can't you believe that? All I am or ever was is a private detective . . ."

"Please," she cried, shaking her head from side to side. "Why say such things? You've known Gloria. While I was telling you about her yesterday you knew the story all along."

"I knew nothing!"

"You've been living with her!"

"The hell I have . . ."

"Don't! the papers are full of it this morning. The whole sordid story!" She was fumbling at her small purse. Then her head was bent forward, her face hidden behind a handkerchief.

The guard was standing there. "I thought I told you no nonsense," he growled at me.

"Leave us alone, will you?" I didn't ask him, I told him.

"You got time to say goodbye," he said. "Make it quick." He turned and walked slowly away. Not as far as he had been, though.

I put my hands on top of the table, palms down, and began counting the fingers. When I looked up she was watching me and there was only a trace of the tears in her eyes.

"I want you to tell me exactly how you think it was," I said quietly.

"What is there to say . . ."

"Just tell it, Kyle."

She seemed to start at the sound of her name. "All right," she said. "You and Gloria have been—in love. You've known her for some time. She told you about my pictures and you took them from my hotel." She took a breath. "That's all there is to it," she said.

"All? How about Gloria? What did I do to her?"

She turned her face. "You killed her," she said. "I don't think it was the way they had it in the papers," she added.

"Why not?"

"I don't think you attacked her," she said softly, still not looking at me. "I don't think you had to."

"Good for me. But why did I kill her?"

Her eyes came around slowly. "I think you were breaking off with her," she said. "I think you . . ."

"You think I *what?*"

"You were going to make a play for me," she said in a swift breath.

"Am I that obvious, Kyle?"

"Please," she said, her voice wavering again. "It was enough yesterday. I . . . I thought about you after you'd left." It was an accusation.

"I'll tell you something. I thought about you."

"Yes," she said. "I guess you did."

"Don't say it like that. I haven't got your pictures. I was looking for them last night when I met Gloria Dennis. It was the first time I'd ever seen her . . ."

"Can't you see how far-fetched that sounds?" she interrupted sharply. "How could you possibly have located a girl who called herself Gaye Dawn unless you knew she was Gloria Dennis and knew exactly where to find her?"

"Because Gaye Dawn was a client of Archie St. George's. That's how I knew."

Her face called me a liar.

"Before you accuse Archie of anything else, Barney, I want to tell you that I called him before I came down here to see you this morning. Archie never heard of her, either as Gaye Dawn or as Gloria."

"He said that?"

"I know he never knew Gloria," she answered. "And when I asked him this morning who Gaye Dawn was he said he didn't know."

"He's a liar, Kyle. He's twice a liar about the same girl . . ."

She lifted her head. "I came to ask you to please give me back the pictures," she said unemotionally. "I don't mean to sound cruel, but they're of no use to you any more. But they are very important to me . . ."

"I don't have them to give, Kyle."

She stared at me for another moment and then quickly stood up. "I was hoping that some part of the man I talked to yesterday was genuine. I didn't believe that you could have fooled me so completely. But you have."

She had already turned toward the guard before I could get to my feet.

"Kyle!"

She was hurrying away and I started after her. The guard stepped in front of me, his arms around me, pinning my own to my sides.

"Don't make it go hard with you, boy!" he shouted in my ear. The door opened and another guard came in. Kyle went past him and out of my sight without turning her head again.

After that scene, the rest of the morning and afternoon dragged slowly. Several times the request came in from the newspapers for question and answer interviews and not less than half a dozen flak-happy lawyers bribed their business cards into my cell. But I wasn't making any statements and I wasn't hiring any Spring Street lawyer.

What did surprise me was the lack of attention from the District Attorney's office. I had expected to spend the day talking to one of the assistants, but lunch and then two o'clock came and went without any word. Then the guard was there, alone, with the news that I was wanted in the interrogation room.

"D.A.?" I asked.

He nodded and took me there.

The fellow behind the worn desk in the room couldn't have been thirty years old. He introduced himself as Assistant District Attorney DeLuca, told me to make myself comfortable in a chair beside the desk and gave me the general impression that he was glad to see me. So this, I thought, is the new approach.

But then a door on the other side of the room opened and the Homicide Lieutenant, Stern, came through. On his heels, unhappy-faced, was Fred Weaver.

Stern nodded to me but Weaver hardly glanced at my face before taking an inconspicuous chair against a wall.

"Why did you play it the hard way, Glines?" Stern asked me suddenly.

What was going on? Had Fred taken my story to Homicide?

"Weaver found Frankie," Stern said. "If you're interested, his last name is Larkin."

I walked over to Fred. "Did you have any trouble with him?"

The detective shrugged. "He took a shot at me," he murmured. "I come near breaking his arm."

"Why didn't you tell us all about him last night?" Stern demanded.

"Come off it, Lieutenant. You had me in a bag and you know it. Anything I'd said about Frankie you'd have fed to the birds. If you did follow it up it might have ended up on the teletype and that Cadillac would have been salted away in some garage for five years. It wasn't a job for a department," I said. "It was strictly a one man investigation."

The young guy from the D.A. spoke. "Evidently you picked the right man," he said. "And to tell you the truth I'm a little surprised at that Cadillac angle."

"There's no reason to be. It was a '56 Fleetwood. The dealers didn't even show them more than five weeks ago. When you figure at least three weeks for delivery, and when you've got the color and the model, finding the owner is no trick. In all the boroughs there are only three Cadillac dealers . . ."

"It was Brooklyn," Fred Weaver said. "But the guy didn't sell it to anybody named Frankie." He stopped and looked around, like a man who thinks he's talking out of turn.

"Finish it for him," said Stern.

Weaver sighed. He hated to use his voice. "I went to the address. It was an apartment out in Brownsville. Crummy neighborhood. But there was this big, shiny black boat parked right out in front. Dumb hoods," he commented sourly. "The name I want is on the third floor. There's a lot of noise behind the door, like a party, but it's not even noon. I ring the bell and the place goes dead. A voice asks me who I am. I say I'm a guy who just run into the Caddy downstairs and I want to square it." Weaver paused to shake his head at the 'dumb hoods.' "Whoosh! the door is open and I'm looking at this punk you told me to pick up. But in the room behind him is a crowd and I don't like their looks so much. So I just grab this Frankie and haul him out of there, slamming the door behind us and off we go. I book him into Bay Ridge and tell them to send a squad back to the apartment. But the place is clean by the time they get there. That crowd left so quick there was a couple of hundred bucks' worth of dope still in the joint."

"Nice," I said. "How about Frankie?"

"Yeh. He's a junkie from the word shoot, Barney. I couldn't get much sense out of him so I brought him back over here to Homicide."

"What did he tell you?" I asked Stern.

"We took him to the laundry," Stern said, meaning that they withheld the addict's regular shot. "It was noisy. It took us two hours to get four coherent sentences out of him. He's at Bellevue now."

"But what did he tell you?"

"That he lifted your .38 and killed the girl. What do you think he told me?"

"You might lose some of that poise," I told him, "if you get tossed in here on a homicide charge."

He smiled. "I'll never lose that," he said, "and I'll never be foolish enough to come as close as you did."

"He's right," the city lawyer chimed in. "I've been busy all morning getting the indictment ready for the grand jury. Even with this Frankie Larkin you'd have been here for two weeks before all the red tape came un-ravelled."

That would have been nice. "Didn't Frankie have any-thing else to say? Any other names?" I asked Stern.

"Listen, Glines. Listen carefully. I just came from a tough time with a crazy hophead. I was working only for you, just the homicide. If there's something else that little maniac has to tell he can tell it to the interested parties. That's you," he added, looking at Weaver. "And, pal, you're welcome to him and his whole family."

"I'm due at Bellevue at five," Fred told me. "It'll prob-ably be a session."

I nodded. I liked it that Stern was bowing out. What Fred Weaver got out of Frankie about the robbery of Kyle's room and the pictures I knew he'd feed to me in full.

"Okay," I said with the nearest thing to cheer in 48 hours, "how do I break out of this pile?"

"You come with me," said the young lad. "We'll sign a few releases and then you're on your own."

"Without apologies from anybody," Stern added.

An hour later I was in a cab, crossing Canal Street and heading north toward that bath, the clean shirt and the old—but pressed—blue flannel with the pin stripe. Then to the Park East Hotel and a long talk with Kyle Shannon.

As long as she knew I was making a play for her there was no more point in being so damned indirect about it.

EIGHT

THERE WAS shock, not mere surprise, in Kyle's voice when she answered the house phone from the lobby. She agreed to see me, but reluctantly, and I knew one of the reasons she didn't want to see me as soon as I crossed the threshold.

Sprawled familiarly in one of the couches, the ever-ready drink in his hand, was Archie St. George. He looked very good in a heavy tweed jacket and gray flannels; very well rested, bright-eyed and every inch the man who knew his way around.

Kyle's voice came from behind me, almost inaudible. "Were you released?"

I smiled and nodded. "I didn't escape, if that's why you look so worried."

"Well tell me what happened. What is it all about?" she sounded warmer, almost relieved.

"They decided they had no case," was all I told her.

"Congratulations," St. George said. "It was hard to believe the story the papers had."

"I'll bet it was, Archie."

He kept his eyes on me for a moment and then got to his feet. "How about a drink, kid?"

"Is it your liquor?"

He smiled. "Now what brings on a crack like that?" he asked over his shoulder and walked to the bar. "You take rye, don't you? With water?"

I nodded and watched him make it. He didn't measure the shot but just tipped the bottle, leaving very little room for water. He was still smiling when he handed it to me.

Kyle came toward us. "It's too early for me," she said, "but let me have a sip of that as a toast." I tilted the glass to her lips and she winced. "*Strong*," she said, eyeing St. George with a sidelong glance.

"Barney likes them that way, don't you, kid?"

"If you say so, kid."

"Now let's hear what happened to you," he said casually "How'd they let you go?"

"There's not much to say, Archie. I told them I didn't do it and then someone dropped into Homicide and told them he did. As simple as that."

"Really? Who's the someone?" He swung around and began walking back to the couch.

"A sweetheart," I said. "A real bird." It was my turn to grin. "They tell me his name is Frankie Larkin." I raised the glass. "And they tell me he's singing his little heart out."

"He confessed?" Kyle asked, standing close to my shoulder, making me take my eyes off St. George's bland face. "This Frankie Larkin killed Gloria?"

"That's what he swears he did," I said.

Her fingers were on my wrist, pressuring it. "I don't know what to say," she told me huskily. "I must have made it pretty terrible for you this morning . . ."

"Forget this morning, Kyle." I pronounced her name carefully. "All that's important is for you to know I'm working for you. I'm going to get your pictures back."

"When?"

That was from St. George.

"Soon, Archie. What time is it now?"

He glanced at the watch on his wrist. "It's four-thirty," he said. "Why?"

"Because that bird, Mr. Larkin, is going into his big act at five." I was enjoying this more than a good night's sleep. I felt good.

"But what has he got to do with my pictures?" Kyle asked, her voice incredulous.

"Larkin is one of the thieves who broke in here, Kyle."

It was getting easier to say her name. I hoped it was getting harder for St. George to hear. "He ought to know what happened to your pictures after they were stolen."

A light was dawning deep in her beautiful eyes.

"That's right," I told her. "Gloria took the pictures that Larkin stole. Larkin came to see Gloria and killed her with my gun."

She was shaking her head again.

"It's not a puzzle," I said. "Is it, Archie?"

"It sounds very far-fetched, now that you ask."

I returned to Kyle. "It wasn't an accident that your pictures were stolen," I said to her. "They knew they were here, and the one who told them about the pictures in the first place was your friend Gloria. She got herself killed because somebody didn't want her talking to me. It was done with my gun because they wanted me to get out of their hair . . ."

"Why not kill you then?" Archie asked quietly.

"If they'd had me killed in the room the investigation would have gone on from there. That would bring a hundred cops into their business instead of the perfect solution of having me railroaded out of circulation. What time is it?" I asked Archie. He'd just glanced at his watch.

"Twenty-five of," he said and got to his feet again. "I've got to get down to Radio City, honey," he told Kyle. "One of my dancers is on the Caesar show and I want to catch the rehearsal." He walked over and kissed her casually on the cheek. Then he cupped her chin and held her face up. "I'll pick you up at eight . . ."

"What kind of a dancer is this client?" I asked.

"Kind?" His voice was annoyed. "What do you mean?"

"What do you think I mean? Does she tap, or do ballet? Or does she strip?"

"I don't like the sound of your voice, Glines. Just what's on your mind?"

"A kid named Gaye Dawn is on my mind. Isn't she on yours?"

"Why should she be?"

"Didn't you book her out of town?"

"No."

"I've got somebody who says you did," I lied.

"No you haven't, Glines. Gaye Dawn was never a client of mine." He came over to me slowly. 'And something else. Kyle here is. My most important client. I'm advising her right now to drop you, professionally and socially and every goddamned way you can think of." As he spoke his voice got tighter. Now his face was white and a nerve jumped high on his cheek. "Get out!"

I grinned, hoping he'd come on. But Kyle stepped between us. "Stop it!" she cried. "Both of you!" She turned to me. "You've got to stop thinking that Archie has anything to do with this terrible business. It's plain you don't like each other," she said, "but that's no reason to make these wild accusations." Then she whirled on him. "And I won't have you running my life, Archie. You've got no call to order Barney out of my home . . ."

"You certainly don't want him around, do you?" he asked.

She looked at me for an instant. "I don't know what I want," she said, shaking her head from side to side. "I wish you'd both leave."

"Okay," I said. "Maybe I'll go down and watch that rehearsal, Archie."

"If you're half as smart as you think you are, Glines, you'll stay as far away from me as you can get."

No matter what he said I couldn't get irritated. My mind was too much on Fred Weaver and the talk he'd soon be having with Frankie Larkin. And it pleased me to watch St. George invent reasons to get out of here. If he thought I wasn't going to stick close to him from now on he'd find out differently as soon as he went out that door.

"What time is it?" I asked him.

But Kyle answered. "It's twenty minutes before five," she said and I watched Archie's face.

"I'll see you later, baby," he said to her and went to the closet for his hat and coat.

The telephone rang.

Kyle moved with long strides to the receiver and lifted it.

"Hello," she said. Then: "Yes, he is." She held the phone to Archie.

"St. George," he said. Then he listened, and as he listened his face grew interested. Finally he said, "It's the only thing to do. I'll see you later." He laid the phone back and when he turned his eyes were on me and he was smiling.

"The rehearsal's been canceled," he said, and that seemed to make his happier. He slipped his arms through the coat and came to Kyle. He kissed her again, this time on the lips. "Eight o'clock," he said. "And wear that red thing. Okay?" His eyes were expressive.

"Oh, it's too formal for just dinner," she said.

"Not where I'm taking you, baby. We're going to do the town tonight."

She gave him a smile that made me catch my breath. "Well," she said. "What brings all this on?"

"I feel like celebrating," he told her. Then, to me: "Too bad you won't be around, Glines."

He started for the door. I said goodbye to the girl and followed him out. I also caught a cab behind his and paid to follow him home. He let himself into his ground floor apartment, closed the door and left me to wait for him.

Five o'clock came and then five-thirty. It was nearly six when I ran out of cigarettes and moved to the drugstore on the corner for a fresh pack. A newspaper truck passed me and a bundle of papers was thrown to the sidewalk beside a stand. I looked down at the latest headlines and there it was: CONFESSES STRIPPER'S MURDER, ESCAPES FROM BELLEVUE!

I had to wait then until the old man unwrapped the bundle and sold me one before learning any more. There wasn't much that the headline bulletin didn't have already. Frankie Larkin, pretending to fall, snatched a policeman's revolver and escaped from the Bellevue criminal ward after seriously wounding two other policemen. The paper noted that he was a drug addict and the police promised his speedy recapture. Sure.

There was also another picture of me and a very quiet, very short story—compared to the big blast this morning —about my release from the Tombs and the dropping of the charges against me.

So that was Archie's telephone call. And I remembered his words. "It's the only thing to do . . ." That could mean only one thing: Frankie Larkin had headed back to the mob. One of the things that would drive him there was the shot of heroin he'd be needing after the tapering-off at the hospital. The other was to try to square himself before too much time went by. And if they killed him when he got to them, that was the chance the poor hophead had to take. Getting dope into his veins was the only thing he cared about.

What now? Bust into Archie's and work him over? No good. Archie wouldn't scare and he knew the spot I'd be in if I pulled a gun on him. A gun I didn't have with me. I would have to get another lead, something else that moved me right up to his front doorstep as Gaye Dawn had.

I thought of the girl in his office, the secretary.

NINE

I was in luck for a change. The night elevator man in Archie St. George's office building was a loose-lipped, dirty-eyed joker who knew the floor, the office and the availability of every woman under forty-five in the place.

"Sure I know her name," he told me, the lips falling away from stained teeth. "But it's gonna cost you."

I laid a dollar bill across his palm.

"I said cost, brother," he said.

I placed a second one in the palm.

"One more," he said. I gave it to him and he said Archie St. George's secretary was Helen Harper. Then he laughed. "You just bought nothing," he said. "That dame is private stock. Strictly for St. George."

But by then I was already on my way out of the place and heading for a public telephone. Helen Harper lived on MacDougal Street in Greenwich Village and I decided on a direct visit without a warning telephone call.

She lived on the fourth floor of a walkup and greeted me with alarm in her eyes and a negligee drawn tightly around her.

"What's happened to Archie?" were the first words out of her mouth.

"Can I come inside and talk to you?"

"Yes!"

I went into her apartment, one-and-a-half rooms and bath, the living room couch doubling as a bed which was made up even this early. "What's happened to him?" she asked again.

I looked at her and said nothing. The trace of yesterday's beating was still on her round, excitingly pretty face.

"Well?"

"Archie's all right," I said.

"Then what do you want?" Suspicion replaced anxiety.

"A talk, Helen."

The familiarity got me nowhere. "About Archie?" she asked.

I nodded and she shook her head.

"If it's about yesterday that's strictly personal. If it's about anything else it's confidential."

I launched a smile. "Suppose it's about both?"

Her stern eyes wiped my face clean. "You're a detective," she said. "I want nothing to do with you." She opened the door to the hall. "I'm sorry," she said, "but that's how it is."

Well, it's a rough business all around. Somebody always does the hurting and somebody always gets hurt. I said: "What I'm here about is not so much Archie but his girl friend."

It hurt. Nice work, Glines.

"His what?" she said, and eyes that had been narrowed were wide enough to hold nickels.

"The redhead," I said. "The beautiful body with all that money."

"Kyle Shannon," she said.

"That's her name."

"What—what did you want to ask me about her?"

I watched her closely. Her face had seemed to lose its color, gone white beneath the makeup. And I stretched an arm out because I thought she was wavering.

"What's wrong?" I said.

She turned her face away. "Nothing . . ." Her voice was limp. Her hand went to her stomach and pressed against it.

"I was wrong when I called her his girl friend," I said, exploring now. I'd wanted a rise out of this girl—but this was too much reaction. "She's only his client . . ."

She didn't hear that. She was moving away from me, heading for the narrow bathroom entrance. Then she was inside and the door was slammed between us.

What would you do? I could only stand there, sick and tired of the wise Barney Glines, and listen carefully for sounds beyond that door as wild thoughts chased each other around my head.

It was easily five minutes when she came back to the room. Came back and headed straight for the convertible couch which she quickly turned back. She was still pale as she sat down but there was an improvement.

"I'm sorry," she said. "Now what did you want to talk to me about?"

There was an improvement, but now I saw how tired she looked. Tired from what? Sitting around Archie St. George's office all day, giving out lies about him on the telephone while he sat in Kyle Shannon's hotel suite? And she's been ready for bed at this hour—a girl who couldn't have been twenty.

"Are you pregnant?" I asked.

She stared back at me out of glassy eyes. Then her vision cleared and she took a deep breath.

"Yes," she said. "If it's any business of yours."

"It isn't," I admitted. "Archie?"

"Yes."

"And when you told him about it yesterday he gave you something else to remember him by . . ."

I stopped abruptly. She sat on the edge of the couch, her body stiffly arched, her head held erect. But beneath the thin wrapper her full breasts heaved dangerously. Then her face fell apart and tears spurted from beneath hopelessly clenched eyelids. I crossed to her, sat down and laid a clumsy, ineffectual arm around her shoulder. That seemed to collapse the rigidity of her and her body turned into mine, the head burrowing against my chest.

"How far gone is it?"

Her answer was muffled by my coat. It sounded like "two months." I kept quiet then and after that first outburst her body seemed to settle itself. The sobbing ceased and she made an effort to straighten up.

"What *did* you come here for?"

"Archie St. George," I said.

"What about him?"

"Anything," I told her truthfully. "Anything at all. I want to hear about him."

"Why?"

"Because I don't like him, Helen. That isn't going to help me with you—but I want you to know I'm against him."

"That's honest," she said. "If I could be honest with myself like that I guess I'd be against him too. But I'm not honest."

"Besides hitting you," I asked, "what did he have to say?"

She closed her eyes. "Not very much. I went into the office and said, 'I have something to tell you, Archie.' He said, 'I'm pretty busy, baby. Can it wait?'" A short bitter laugh escaped her throat. "It couldn't wait," she said to me. "Then I told him I was pregnant. Do you know what he said?"

I shook my head.

"He said, 'That's tough sailing, doll.' He said, 'Who's the lucky guy?' Those were his words, *who's the lucky guy!*" Her voice went up sharply.

"That," she went on, "was my first notice about the other Archie. I told him—a little hysterically, I guess—that he was the only man in New York it could be. He'd been reading some letter while we talked, not even glancing at me. Then he looked up and his eyes went right through me. All the way through. 'So?' he said. 'What do you want me to do about it?'"

She was living it again. I wasn't here with her as Barney Glines—just someone, anyone; a pair of ears. "What did I want him to do about it?" she said. "I wanted him to be the person who'd taken me out, who'd bought me so many presents, who told me how beautiful I was. I wanted him to marry me," she said.

I stood up. "I'm leaving," I explained to her. "I shouldn't have come and I'm sorry that I broke in on your troubles with my own."

"No!" She came to her feet and the gown partly closed itself. "You said something about Kyle Shannon."

"That was a mistake."

"Why was it a mistake?"

"It's got nothing to do with you and Archie."

"It has everything to do with us. He's in love with her," she said. "Just the way he says her name when he has me call her . . . He does love her, doesn't he?"

"You know as much— You know more about the man than I do," I said to her. All I wanted to do now was leave.

"He couldn't help being in love with her," she said quietly. "No man could . . ." Her eyes raised to mine knowingly. "Oh," she said. "That's why you're here. You're in love with her too!"

"That isn't why I'm here."

"Then why are you? What do you want me to tell you?"

"Nothing."

"Is it about Gloria?"

"What?"

"The girl you were with last night. The one that fellow killed—the one who escaped."

"You're up on everything," I told her.

She laughed. "Who isn't? When I saw your face at the door my knees went weak."

"But all you thought about was Archie," I reminded her. "Why?"

"Because of Gloria," she answered quickly. "Gloria was Archie's client."

"You know that?"

"Know it? She was up there almost every day. Then she went out of town."

"When?"

"I don't know," she said. "A few months ago."

"Did Archie get her a job outside of New York?"

She nodded. "He made up a complete tour. I remember how hard he worked on it, calling people all over the country for weeks. The phone bills alone were three hundred dollars."

"What was so important about booking her out of town?"

Helen Harper smiled sadly. "Her career. It's always good when you've flopped in New York to go on the grand tour. Las Vegas, Los Angeles, New Orleans, Miami Beach. Then you come back and your agent has a sales story." She walked to a small table, took a cigarette from its pack and lit it. "Except for one thing," she went on. "I think Gloria was sent on the tour for another reason." She blew a cloud of blue smoke into the room. "Gloria," she said easily, "was the mistress before me. But it wasn't me that made Archie send her away."

"Why did he?"

She came back to me slowly. "You saw Kyle Shannon yesterday," she said. "The fur coat, the dress, the way her hair was done. She was a little breathtaking." Her eyes scanned my face for a reaction. I tried to give her none. "I saw her another way," Helen Harper said. "I saw pictures of her and she didn't look quite the way she did yesterday."

"Where did you see the pictures?" I asked.

"They were in Archie's desk. Gloria had come in and they left together for lunch. I had to go into his desk for a letter that had come in and had been stuck away in there. What I found were pictures of her in the nude. I don't know what she was trying to do. She looked almost like she was—I don't know . . ."

"Modeling," I said.

Her head came up. "Yes! That's it, she was modeling. Have you seen them?"

I shook my head. "Where are the ones you saw?"

"That was my first and last look at them. Right after

that Gloria was on her tour. But," she said, "from the little I heard and the little I could guess, I think Archie made her leave town on account of those pictures."

"Why do you think that?"

"Kyle Shannon was an important client. She was up for a picture. Somehow or other, Gloria Dennis was connected with those pictures. Archie didn't want her around."

"Tell me," I said, "did Archie ever give that girl any drugs?"

She took a step backward.

"Did he?"

"I wouldn't know anything about that," she said.

"Did he ever give you any?"

She shook her head.

"Did he try?"

"Once," she said. "He had a package of marijuana cigarettes. I told him I didn't want one. Not ever."

"How about himself?" I asked. "Did he smoke them?"

"No," she said. "I never saw him. Why are you asking me about drugs?"

"I'm trying to get a picture of the guy," I told her frankly.

"Why? What has he done to you?"

"He's used me," I said quietly.

"Oh." She walked away from me. "He seems to be good at using people." Her back was to me and her voice seemed muted. "He's pretty serious about Kyle Shannon, isn't he?" she asked.

There was no point now in making her feel good.

"Yes," I said. "But it isn't going to do him any good."

She turned. "Why?"

"Because Archie is into something that's swallowing him."

"What has he done?"

"Nothing that you can do anything about, Helen. Archie just happens to be one of those people who do nothing with their lives but spread bad news. You don't really want to marry him, do you? You're not in love with him?"

"No, not in love. But I've been hit pretty hard."

"You've got plenty of living ahead of you," I said. "The smart thing to do is just chalk the year 1956 off your calendar."

"You make it sound simple," she said bitterly.

"Of course it isn't simple! But what are you going to do, spend the rest of your life regretting an affair that couldn't have worked out from the start?"

"No," she said. "I guess not . . ."

"How do you feel about having the baby?"

"I'm scared to death."

"Don't do anything foolish," I warned her. "Stay away from those butchers who call themselves abortionists. And don't start jumping off the bed or any of those things. Are you listening?"

"Yes."

I took one of my cards from my wallet and wrote a name and address on it. "Here," I said, handing her the card. "This doctor is a close friend of mine. He's up in Hanover, New Hampshire. You go up there now and he'll see that you have a nice job until it's time to have the baby. When it's born you can decide whether to keep it or have him place it for you."

"Why are you doing all this for me?"

"If I'm doing anything I'm trying to make amends for the thing that happened to Gloria last night. I'll call the doctor in the morning and tell him to expect you before the week is out. Okay?"

She almost smiled. "Okay," she said.

"And I'll make a bet with you, beautiful. One year from tonight you'll be married to somebody who loves you and all of this will never have happened at all."

"Sure," she said, trying to sound as if she believed it.

"And as for St. George—"

"Never mind him!" she snapped. "And I think you'd better go now."

"All right. But don't let that heel get you down. He isn't worth worrying about."

"I want you to go," she said. "I don't want any man near me. Never again."

"You are going up to Hanover, aren't you?"

She nodded absently.

There was nothing more I could say, nothing I could do. I opened the door, murmured a good night and left.

When I closed Helen Harper's door I was all out of strings with Archie St. George's name on them. All that was left to me was a killer named Frankie Larkin—and as sure as one and one makes two he was nothing but a walking dead man. If he was still walking.

The one who would hear about it first was Stern and I called him at West 20th Street.

"Where the hell have you been?" was his greeting.

"Why?"

"Your friend Larkin has turned up dead. He was gunned in a stolen car and left at Coney Island."

"What kind of leads do you have?"

"A beauty," the man from Homicide said. "They never did tumble to that Cadillac business. We have the bird who actually bought the car and he's rattled. Gave us three stories about where he was tonight and not one of them stands up. Why don't you come down and take a look at him? He may be the other lad from last night."

"I'm on my way," I said and arrived five minutes later. The man they had was named Albie Warner but he wasn't the one who'd held a gun on me while Frankie shot Gloria Dennis.

I shook my head at Stern.

"Never saw him at all?" he asked me.

"No. Does he ever say anything?"

"Not for the last half hour he hasn't. Albie," he said to the suspect, "tell us a funny story."

Albie made as though to spit but no words came from his lips.

"Go on, sweetheart. Give us the story of your life."

Albie was watching me and I knew that he had made me as the contact man for Kyle Shannon's jewels. Albie might have been the voice giving directions on the phone. But he wasn't talking and from the looks of him he wasn't planning to. Not, at least, for my pleasure. And I wasn't going to start pumping him about Archie St. George— not until the pictures were back in Kyle's hands and the chips could fall as they damned pleased. It was a stand-off and I wanted to leave. The Police Department would solve the murder of Frankie Larkin, not me. And they wouldn't open up on Albie Warner while a civilian private investigator was around.

"I can't help you with him, Lieutenant," I said.

"Thanks for coming down, anyway," he said politely. "We'll eventually get a story out of this one that will add up."

"I'm sure you will," I said and went out of the station house.

Stern would get his story all right, slowly, over a couple of hours that would be tiring for him, the squad and for Albie Warner. And then the net would go out for the rest of the mob—men who were fleeing in all directions right now or as soon as they heard Albie had been picked up.

What about Archie St. George? It was eight-thirty now and if he was already out with Kyle Shannon the chance of hearing about Warner was not probable. But when he did hear, what would he do? What would I do? It would depend on how much Albie Warner knew about the whole racket—on how tightly he could connect St. George by direct evidence and not hearsay. New York State makes it tough to prove a conspiracy, as a lot of policemen have learned. It takes the testimony of a non-conspirator, a neutral third party, to turn the trick.

If there wasn't a non-conspirator, Archie could just deny Warner's story and sit tight. But there *was* someone who could tie him into Kyle's pictures—and as soon as

St. George found out that Warner had been picked that someone was in trouble.

I ducked into an 8th Avenue drugstore and called Helen Harper. The phone rang. And rang. And rang. I slammed the hook down, collected the dime and put in a fast call to the 5th Precinct. I gave the cop her name, address and floor and told him to please hurry. Then the Park East Hotel.

"No," said the desk clerk, "Miss Shannon has just left the hotel. Is this Mr. St. George?"

"No! Why should it be?"

He didn't like my tone but I couldn't help that.

"Because," he told me icily, "Miss Shannon left a message for Mr. St. George if he should call."

"What message?"

"I'm very sorry, sir . . ." he began officiously and I hung up on him. No answer at Helen Harper's. St. George hadn't come by for Kyle at eight. I flagged a cab and headed him toward MacDougal Street.

Two parked police cars forced us to stop several houses away from the girl's flat. There were people milling on the sidewalk around the entrance. There were more patrols further down, an ambulance. One policeman was planted in the entranceway, keeping people in and keeping people out.

I was one he wanted to keep out.

"My name is Glines . . ."

"The word is to beat it," he said.

"Just tell me what's wrong."

"I'm telling you to move on . . ."

"Is it a girl?" I asked. "On the fourth floor?"

That interested him. "That's right. What do you know about it?"

"What's happened to her?"

"She died."

Oh, God! "How? What happened?"

An insistently blaring horn interrupted us and I turned to see a black sedan pushing its way through the congestion on the street. Both doors opened and four men piled out. The second one on the sidewalk was Stern and the one behind him was Bradley.

His eyes widened at the sight of me.

"What are you doing here?"

"I was the one who sent for the cops," I said emptily. "Just like last night."

"Yeah. Who is it tonight?"

"I think it's a kid named Harper."

"Let's go up and see," he said. Stern had nothing against me except annoyance about last night. But he waited for me to turn and proceed him up the four flights of stairs.

Helen Harper's door was closed. I opened it to find several uniformed policemen, an ambulance driver and a whitejacketed interne. He was bent over the couch that was a bed again and on it was the naked—cruelly uncovered—body of Helen Harper.

The young doctor straightened up and looked at all of the new faces for the one that would be in charge.

"What is it, Doctor?" Stern asked softly, coming out of our group and walking toward him.

"Death," he said, spreading his hands eloquently.

"From what?" asked the detective, his voice deferential.

The man in white shook his head. "I wouldn't want to say," he said. "You've sent for the examiner?"

"What do you think it is?" Stern persisted.

"Come here," the doctor said. He stooped down and lifted Helen Harper's arm from the bed. "She seems to have had her arm punctured by a needle," he said cautiously.

I moved in closer at that. Sure enough, there was a familiar cluster of needle marks on her forearm.

A uniformed man came up to Stern. He held a metal hypodermic syringe in his hand.

"I was the first one in here, Lieutenant," he said. "She was just like you see her now and this damn thing was on the floor."

"Where?" It came out of me without thinking. The last thing I wanted to do was ask questions at an official party like this one.

The cop mistook me for a glamour boy.

"Right here, sir," he said, pointing to a spot on the floor just beside the bed.

"Why?" Stern asked me.

"I'm not sure," I said. "I didn't think she was a junkie."

"Did you see her arm?"

I nodded. "You think she was killed by morphine?" I asked the doctor.

"I think absolutely nothing," he answered positively. "This is your business, police business. Let your medical examiner tell you what she died of."

Hell, I'd gone this far. "Why don't you get rid of that stiff neck?" I asked him. "If this girl was your sister what would she be dead from?"

He didn't take offense. "If that were the case, God forbid, then this girl was killed by a tremendous entrance of some cocaine derivative into her blood stream." He spoke pedantically but it was obvious that it was natural with him. He was young and filled with self-importance, an attitude I'd seen before with internes and new-capped nurses trying to cover up their awe.

Then he said: "And I'm inclined to go along with your theory that this girl was not an addict."

"Why?" asked Stern.

"Her complexion, for one thing. And notice her pupils," he added, extending an arm toward the staring eyes. "They're distended from the quantity of drug but they're not opaque. Number three," he said, "these needle wounds are fresh, very fresh. I would say they are not an hour old."

Not an hour old. Not one of them an hour old. I knew then for sure that Helen hadn't given herself the shots. It was someone else. Helen had been planning on Hanover when I left her. And it hadn't been just a cute act, either. She was going. And like a damn fool, she'd called

St. George to kiss him off for good, and she'd told him that I'd been there. Or else he had called her. Either way, he'd found out about me.

"How long has she been dead?" Stern wanted to know.

"Less than an hour," the doctor answered. "But no more opinions." He reached down and picked up his black bag. "My name is Benkert," he said. "I'll have my report for you at the hospital in the morning."

"Thank you, Doctor," the policeman told him. Then he turned to his squad. "Get to work," he told them. To me, he said: "Let's have it, Glines, and fast."

I wanted to give him the whole story, the works. But I also wanted to be the hell out of Greenwich Village and on the trail of Kyle Shannon. If this was Archie St. George's work, then he was getting desperate. The wraps were off and I had to get between him and Kyle Shannon. "This girl knew the one from last night. Gloria. I saw her about seven o'clock and stayed for ten or fifteen minutes. She asked me to get out and I did."

"What brought you back?"

"I was worried about her. Especially after last night. When I left your place I called here. There was no answer so I asked the precinct to look into it. Then I came down by cab."

"What is this thing you're working on?" Stern asked gently. "What's it all about?"

I sighed.

"Don't get me wrong," he said. "It's a citizen's privilege to hire a private detective and be entitled to privacy. Providing it's restricted to the citizen's private business . . ."

"What I'm doing doesn't involve my client in this," I told him.

"You know what I hate?" he asked me surprisingly. "I hate *private* detectives. They make the hair stand up on my spine. But you know something else?"

He waited and I said, "What?"

"I like you. I've been involved with private detectives

half a dozen times over the years, but never like I'm involved with you. But still I like you. How do you figure that?"

"I don't know," I admitted. "But I'm still not telling you what I'm working on or who I'm working for."

He smiled. "See right through me, don't you, you son of a bitch? All right, go on to wherever you're in such a hurry to get to."

"Thanks," I said.

"And when you get there," he called after me, "save time and call me first. Skip the local precinct."

I walked clear to 5th Avenue before I found another phone. No, he told me, Miss Shannon hadn't returned. No, there was no message for a Barney Glines.

Then I started calling the likely places she might be for dinner. She was not at *The Colony,* not at *21,* not at the *Stork,* not at *Shor's,* not at *Armando's*—a suave voice said, yes, Miss Shannon had been at the *Persian Room.* She had left fifteen minutes ago with Mr. Archie St. George. I thanked him.

Another try at the hotel, a ten minute cab ride from Central Park South. She had not returned. Where was she? She was with Archie St. George and my stomach was a hard knot that would never come untangled.

I got in a cab and told him to take me home. The gun they'd used to kill Gloria Dennis was in the District Attorney's office. But there was another one sunken beside the cushion of my leather chair. I wanted to have it in my hand very much.

TEN

I SAT in my room and chain smoked. There was no light on and my hand didn't stray six inches from the telephone beside my chair. In the next two hours I made the rounds again twice, adding the *Copa, Latin Quarter,* half a dozen of the better strip clubs and any place that came to my mind where they might have gone.

At midnight she had still not returned to her hotel and the only thing left to do was go over there and stake myself out in the lobby until she did. If she did. I dropped into Tommy Parise's, as much to see a familiar face as to take on a two-drink fortification for what might turn out to be a long night. And when I arrived at the Park East the night man had a message for me.

"Miss Shannon arrived just after your last call," he said.

"Alone?"

He cleared his throat. "There was a gentleman with her," he admitted. "Mr. St. George."

I picked up the house phone.

"They've left again," he said.

"They *what?*"

He looked like a man who would rather stop talking. But he said: "Miss Shannon had a traveling case with her."

"Did you speak to her?" I shouted at him. "Did you tell her I'd been trying to get her all night."

He nodded. "Yes, I did, Mr. Glines."

"What did she say? Talk, will you?"

"She didn't say much at all. She just nodded her head as though she'd expected you to call. Then she murmured

93

something that I didn't quite make out. Something to the effect that you were right . . ."

"What were her words?"

"Let me think," he said. "This might have been it: 'He was right about everything and I was wrong.' Then Mr. St. George took her arm and they left. Rather hurriedly, as a matter of fact."

By then I was leaving, rather hurriedly. It was one-fifteen that morning when I turned up her name on a passenger list of an Eastern Airlines plane to Palm Beach. And yes, there *was* a Mr. Archie St. George aboard the same plane. It had left at 12:25. The next flight? 4 A.M.

I stepped off the plane and into a summery Florida morning at 8:15. A cab took me into Palm Beach itself and I began a hotel-by-hotel search for them. But there was no Kyle Shannon and no Archie St. George registered. Nor did any of several dozen bellhops remember a tall and beautiful redhead.

I got into another cab and explained my problem to the driver.

"If they're not in any of the hotels in town," he said, believing my story about my best friend and my wife, "you can try the cabins along the beach."

We did—and at the third stop the old man in the renting office had let a cabin the night before to a man from New York and his wife. The wife was redhaired, all right, but they were Mr. and Mrs. Russell, not St. George.

"What cabin?" I asked as casually as I could.

"Well, now. I'm not sure as I ought to tell you that, mister. This is a very respectable place here. We don't want any troublemakers . . ."

I pulled him close to me, my fingers on the collar of his flowered sport shirt. "You're going to have all kinds of trouble here if you don't give me their cabin."

"I don't want any . . . *Okay!* Take it easy, mister. The Russells are in Seabreeze . . ."

"Where the hell is Seabreeze?"

"Don't get so damn excited," he complained. "It's the yellow cottage. Down near the beach path."

I let him go and headed for the yellow cottage. I was almost running. From the outside it looked quite large, at least three, maybe four rooms. Leading up to the white door was a short flight of steps. The door was locked, but it was frail and even as I pushed gently I felt it give. I laid my shoulder against the top, my knee against the bottom and shoved hard. It opened noiselessly and let me into a small, square living room whose windows were darkened by tightly closed blinds. There was no one here. Across the room was another closed door. I moved to it, drawn by a small sound from the other side.

It was a woman's voice, not speaking but softly crying. I turned the knob and this door was locked.

"Who's there?" asked Archie St. George viciously.

"A visitor," I told him. "Open up."

"Barney!" That was Kyle who'd cried my name. Did she really sound happy, or was I wishing it?"

"Get out of here, Glines. Fast." He was standing less than a foot from me, but there was a door between us that I didn't dare break open.

"You don't want me to leave, Archie," I told him. "If I do I'll come back with some law. You don't want that."

There was a noise above my head and I looked to see a narrow glass transom being opened.

"Throw your gun in here," he ordered.

I took the .38 from my jacket and reluctantly pushed it through the transom. Then the door was unlocked.

"Come on in," he said and his voice was from further away.

I went in. Kyle was on one of the twin beds, her back propped against the headboard, a sheet held at her throat. Her eyes were drawn and tired, her cheeks were pale and tearstained, her red-blonde hair was a shambles—but there was a warm smile of welcome on her lips at the sight of me.

He was off to one side, barefoot, wearing nothing but

shorts. Behind him on a table, beside an almost empty quart of Dewar's, was my .38. In his hand was an Army .45 automatic, a hand that shook dangerously.

"Over there," he said, waving me toward the other bed. I went to it. "Sit down." I sat.

"You shouldn't have come here, Barney," Kyle said. "This is my problem . . ."

"How much do you know about all this?" I asked her, ignoring him.

"Only that he has the pictures," she said. "He got them back from the jewel thieves."

"Got them back? He's one of them, Kyle. Archie is the one . . ."

"Shut up!"

I didn't turn my head. "Archie sent them to your hotel. He knew about the pictures because he'd been living with Gloria Dennis. Gloria must have told him all about you . . ."

She swung around to face him. "I know how terrible you are, Archie. But I didn't think you could be that rotten!"

"Glines is a liar," he snarled. "I never laid eyes on anybody named Gloria!"

"He brought me into it," I said, "to prove how valuable he was in your life. After I fell on my face he'd go out and get the pictures back himself. But before you got them he'd ask you politely to marry him. If you said yes then everything would be fine. If you said no . . ."

"Glines, so help me God . . ."

"You won't squeeze that thing, Archie. You're still too busy trying to figure out an angle without adding me to the list." I spoke to Kyle again. "If you turned down his proposal you get this treatment. Isn't that how it worked?"

She nodded.

"But you're not going to marry him, Kyle."

"The hell she isn't!"

"I am, Barney. I have a very clear picture of how

Archie St. George can hurt me if he doesn't get his own way. And after last night it doesn't matter much one way or another."

"You're breaking my heart," St. George sneered. "Okay, Glines, you've heard the lady say it. Now pick up and get out of my life."

"I'm not going anywhere, Archie," I told him, getting slowly to my feet. It had taken a lot out of me to sit there and speak calmly, to listen to him and look at Kyle and the bed and her clothes strewn around the floor where he must have ripped them from her body. I stood up and felt the blood race through me. "I'm not going anywhere," I said again, and moved toward him. "I came down here to kill you."

The gun was raised, its barrel slanting upward toward my neck.

"You won't use that, Archie. You've still got a chance to beat the New York rap. Unless somebody saw you go to the Harper girl's room it'll go down on the books as accidental death from an overcharge of morphine. Albie Warner's a hood. If he mentions your name at all it'll be your word against his . . ."

He had backed up to the wall and I kept coming,

"But if I get shot there's a detective named Stern who'll be on your back for the rest of your life. I'll be the link that ties you to all of it, Archie."

"Don't come any closer, Glines."

His knuckle was white under the trigger-guard. Either I had figured this man right or I would be dead in the next five seconds. I took the step that would bring me close enough to touch him.

And I was right!

"I'll make a deal!"

"No."

"Barney!" It was Kyle, a voice and a blur of white flesh leaping from the bed and throwing herself against me, out of the way of the gun.

Her arms holding me and steadily pushing me away.

I was partly turned from St. George and unable to do anything about it when he brought the .45 down on the back
of my skull. My knees buckled but I didn't go down.
Kyle was screaming into my ear and trying to keep St.
George from hitting me again.

I put my hands on her naked waist and pushed her out
of the line. St. George cracked me across the cheek with
the butt of the .45 and I grabbed it and drove my right
fist deep into his body.

"Hold it!"

It was a new voice, from the doorway and very loud. I
kept on hitting St. George and getting hit.

"I said hold it, goddamnit!"

This time the voice was right on top of me and two
strong and capable arms had mine pinned to my side
from the rear.

"What in hell's going on in here?" I've heard enough
angry policemen all my life to recognize this as one now.
I let my body relax and he released me, stepping between
us.

"Let's have that pistol," he roared and snatched it out
of Archie's fingers. "Go get some clothes on, young lady.
What the hell's going on here?"

Kyle, seeming to notice herself for the first time,
quickly snatched the sheet from the bed, wrapped it
around her and then picked up her suitcase and went with
it to the other room. In the doorway was the clerk from
the renting office, glaring at me accusingly.

"This is a respectable place," he said. "We don't have
troublemakers . . ."

"Who are you?" the policeman asked me.

"Barney Glines. New York."

"Naturally," he answered. "Where else does Palm
Beach get trouble from? Well, my name is Fred Turkus
and I'm just the man to look for when you want to start
anything down here." He swung to Archie. "Who are
you?"

"My name is Russell," he said. "John Russell."

"New York?"

"Los Angeles," he lied again.

Turkus had no quarrel with Los Angeles. "This your pistol?"

Archie nodded.

"What the hell were you trying to do with it?"

"I was trying to get this man to leave," he said truthfully enough.

"All right," said Turkus, swinging back to me. "What did you want in here? From the looks of that front door, you busted in. What the hell's the idea?"

I looked at Archie. He was Mr. John Russell from Los Angeles. The clerk would back him up on that and he might even have some phoney identification with him. And Kyle was Mrs. John Russell—and I had no way of being sure whether she would still go along with that.

"It was a mistake," I said. "I thought Mr. Russell was somebody else. We started fighting . . ."

"Who'd you think he was?"

What would he believe? I said, "I thought he was a friend of mine who ran off with my wife."

"Well, now," said Fred Turkus understandingly. "I'm as sorry as I can be to hear that, mister. But still and all you had no call to come invading Mr. Russell's privacy."

"I'll apologize," I said.

"How about my front door?" complained the clerk.

"I'll pay for it," I said.

"Fine!" said the policeman, or sheriff, his face beaming. "Now what do you say we leave Mr. and Mrs. Russell to themselves."

High heels clicked at the doorway and we all turned to see Kyle standing there, still somewhat disheveled but dressed in blouse and skirt.

"It's all been straightened out, Miz Russell," he told her paternally. "Sorry for all the trouble and for speaking so sharp there a moment ago. Didn't know it was a simple misunderstanding."

Kyle stared at him blankly.

"I want to apologize too, Mrs. Russell," I said quickly. "Maybe you and your husband will let me buy you some breakfast?"

"That's the way to end these things," agreed Turkus. "Everybody get friendly and enjoy Palm Beach. It's a shame and a disgrace to waste all this beautiful paradise on trouble and anger."

"The restaurant's open for breakfast now," the clerk chimed in.

"Good," I said. "I'll see you both over there." I turned to Archie and smiled.

We left the cottage then and I went to the restaurant. From a table on the porch I could see anything that went on in the yellow house. If they weren't out of there within fifteen minutes I was going back in.

It was Kyle who came out, alone. I watched her cross the rich green lawn, her head high, her legs striding with a particular confidence that I was coming to think of as hers alone. She stopped beneath a young palm tree, the two of them making quite a picture, and looked around for me. Then our eyes met and she waved and came on.

She was still smiling, surprisingly happy and light-hearted-looking as I helped her into a seat at the table.

"Everything's going to work out," she said. Her hand rested atop mine and her fingers squeezed for a moment. "Oh, Barney, what a sight you were coming through that door! But what in heaven's name were you trying to do? He would have killed you in another second . . ."

I smiled at her and shook my head. "What do you mean everything's going to work out?"

"He's willing to make a deal with you—with us." Her eyes sparkled in her face. "With us," she repeated.

"He's in no spot to be making deals," I said. "Did you understand any of what I was trying to tell you over in the cottage? St. George is involved in two murders. Three, if you count what happened to Frankie Larkin . . ."

"Please," she said. "I don't want to think of all that's

happened. All I know is that he's asking you to give him twenty-four hours. Let him get away."

"Nothing doing, Kyle."

"And he'll return the pictures," she said.

"When?"

"He'll check them someplace now and mail the check to me in twenty-four hours. If you let him get away."

"No. I'm going to kill him . . ."

"But you can't, Barney! You can't kill him because of me. Don't you see what it would do to us?"

I stared at her. She had said it, not me.

"Barney, this has been the worst series of days and nights either of us will ever live through again. From the moment that man told me on the phone to contact Barney Glines to get my things back I've been tossed and twisted every which way. I heard your name and I hated you for being a thief. I saw you the next day and I hated you even more for looking and talking like you do and turning all these wonderful qualities toward crime. Then you came to see me with the jewelry. Remember?"

"Yes, I remember."

"You told me about your father. That was all I needed, Barney. No man had ever hit me like you had. All it took to fall in love with you was one little push." She took an emotional breath. "Then I see the papers next morning. Were you the man I'd fallen in love with the night before? I cried, Barney, until I was exhausted. When I stopped I hated you again—but much worse because I felt so much involved with you. Can you understand that, Barney?"

"I can understand it, Kyle. It's almost too much for me to believe, though. What you're saying now is what I feel about you. It's why I can't take the idea of St. George being allowed to live . . ."

"He's nothing to us, Barney. Not any more! Our horrible week is over, it was a nightmare. We've got our lives to forget him in. Our whole lives, darling! What does he mean to us?"

"You say our lives, Kyle. Do you mean if I asked you to marry me you would?"

"If you asked me."

"I'll give him the twenty-four hours," I said.

"What about us?"

"I want to see what he'll give us, Kyle. I've got to find out if I'm wrong about St. George's idea of a bargain."

"Oh." Her voice was subdued.

"You'd better go over there and tell him," I said. "If I got in the same room with him again . . ."

She got up from her chair quickly, her face averted. "You'll be back to have breakfast?"

She turned. "Do you want me to, Barney?"

I stood up and put my hands on her shoulders.

"You don't understand, Kyle."

"I understand that you don't want to marry me," she said.

"That's what I mean. You tell that— Tell St. George to do his little trick with your pictures and then to get going. Tell him . . ."

"Tell him what?"

"Nothing," I said. "He won't have to be told."

She turned and retraced her steps to the cottage, walking, I noted unhappily, without that marvelous spring in her legs. But there was nothing for it. If Archie St. George reneged I'd find him and kill him if it took the rest of my life. And Kyle was right—we couldn't live together with that between us.

ELEVEN

I BOARDED the noon plane to New York with
Kyle and it was five o'clock when the cab arrived at the
Park East Hotel.

I walked with her past a saucer-eyed desk clerk to the
elevators.

"Aren't you coming up, Barney?"

"There are some people I want to talk to," I said, meaning Stern and Fred Weaver.

"How about dinner?"

"I don't know when I'll be through with them," I said.

"Meaning you don't want to see me tonight?"

"No, Kyle. That isn't what I mean. Nothing like it."

"But you can't put Archie out of our lives?"

"Not just like that. It's a little more than turning off a
television set."

"All right," she said. "But you're not going to sit some-
where and brood tonight, are you? You're not going to get
on a plane and go back down there again?"

"No," I said, "I'm not going to do that. For all we know
Archie may be right here in New York. The last I saw of
him he was taking his bag into a Palm Beach taxicab and
driving off. He could be almost anywhere tonight."

"But you and I are right here," she said, standing very
close to me and refusing to believe that St. George wasn't
gone and forgotten.

"It'll take me a little while to get used to that," I said.

"Used to what?"

"That it's you and me. No agent."

"I want to get used to it, too," she said urgently. "In my
own way, not yours," she added and her arms were

around my neck and I was kissing her for the first time.
We stopped and she looked around, smiling brightly.

"Now it's official," she told me in a low voice. "Look at
all the witnesses."

"I really should talk to these people," I said.

"You'll come over as soon as you can?"

"I'll call you."

"Be sure," she said. "It's very important, darling."

She spoke very seriously just then.

"Is something wrong, Kyle?"

She shook her head mysteriously. "It's something that
has to be set right," she said. "And soon!" Then she was
in the elevator and the door was closing.

The evening papers were giving the death of Frankie
Larkin the deluxe ride, still running near-naked publicity
stills of Gloria Dennis along with mug shots of Larkin and
Albie Warner. Stern had apparently been very tight with
the real story—or as much of it as *he* knew—because one
paper was bannerlining a wild 'inside' tale that billed
Gloria as Larkin's "moll" who had been killed because
she two-timed him for Warner. Warner had then killed
Larkin when the escaped killer came gunning for him
etc. etc. continued on page ten.

I was—thank God—the forgotten man. To cover up their
slight error of two mornings ago they were ignoring me
completely. But nowhere in any of the papers did I read
that Warner had talked. Nor had any of the others been
picked up.

I called Stern to find out and he admitted that they
had three names from Albie Warner but no line on where
the men were.

Then he named them. No Archie St. George.

"What I want, Glines, is some straight talk on that
Harper girl. Did you know, for instance, that she was
two months pregnant?"

"Yes," I admitted.

"Well?"

"Don't 'well' me, Lieutenant. I'm not the man."

"Who is?"

"I don't know," I told him. "I got to her the same way I got to Gloria Dennis."

"Which was . . . ?"

"A private investigation," I answered.

"Okay, Glines," he said quietly. "I have on my desk an official complaint against you and a Police Department request that your license in this State be revoked. If you listen closely you'll hear me sign it. It'll be on the Attorney General's desk at nine o'clock tomorrow morning."

"Can you hold it?"

"How long?"

"Twenty-four hours."

"It's a deal."

"Thanks, Stern."

"For what?"

He had me there so I hung up.

Fred Weaver had gone off duty at four o'clock, I was told, and my call found him home.

"I'll buy you a dinner," I told him and went up to his Yorkville neighborhood where I met him in a *brauhaus*. Over a plate of thick roast beef and three beers I told him some more of the story that I had begun in the Tombs. I said "girl" when I meant Kyle and "louse" when I meant Archie St. George.

"You could have broken up the whole thing right at the start," he told me sadly.

"Maybe. But I didn't. The reason I'm talking to you is because of the girl. If I laid it on Stern's desk he'd drag her into the homicide angle and that's exactly what I can't let happen."

"You're not God," he said.

"Neither are Homicide Lieutenants."

"So?"

"So Stern has nothing but names. His case is freezing

right under him because the boys who own those names are holed up tight. Where, Fred?"

He laughed. "I give up, where?"

"Do you think they've left town?"

"Not if they're New York punks. They've got a better chance right here than some other city where they have to ask directions to get to a john."

"I think you're right. And I also think they've gone to a hotel. God, how you can lose yourself in a hotel!"

He nodded.

"Okay," I said. "And we know they have some kind of connections at the Leewood and the Barnet down at 33rd. Do you think your boss could be convinced into a stakeout at both places?"

"We got a new captain," he said. "Just promoted. I think I could talk to him." He leaned back and wiped his face with a napkin. "Except for one thing, Glines. Stern wants those babies, not Robbery."

"Like hell. These are pros, Fred. A well organized heist mob. When you talk to them you'll have a lot of your problems solved."

"I did talk to the one Stern has," the detective said. "That didn't help me any."

"Okay," I sighed, looking around for a waiter. "It was just an idea."

"Relax, son. I'll call the precinct now. Have a little apple pie for me when I get back, will you?"

Fred Weaver's boss was willing to try it for twelve hours. And, from what Fred said, he didn't care much one way or another about stepping on Homicide's tender toes.

It was almost nine o'clock when I got back to my apartment, saw how worn out I looked, and went to the phone to wish Kyle a goodnight. The thing rang in my hand before I could pick it up to dial.

"Barney, can you come right over?" It was a Kyle I had never heard before.

"What's happened?"

"That man called. The one who told me to get in touch with you the night my jewels were stolen."

"What did he want?"

"Money. He said he had to have fifty thousand dollars by nine o'clock tomorrow morning. Barney . . ."

"What?"

"He said he'd just been talking by long distance phone to Archie . . ." Her voice faded away, leaving a roaring sound in my ears. "Barney? Are you there?"

"I'm here."

"I need you with me, darling. More than you need to find Archie."

That brought me out of it. "I'm on my way. Don't open the door to anyone until you hear my voice. It has to be my voice, do you understand?"

"Yes, Barney. But . . ."

"But nothing. I'll be there as fast as I can. Just don't open that door until I do."

We hung up and I called Fred Weaver's boss. I told him who I was and what had happened.

"Good," he said. "It proves they're in New York. I haven't had word from any of the men at the hotels."

"But you might, Captain. This mob knows that I'm going to do what I can to take care of the girl. They also know I'm not going to let her hand over any fifty thousand dollars, now or next month."

"And?"

"That's getaway money they're after, Captain. It's something they've got to have to buy their way out— and they need it fast. What they're surely going to do is try to keep me away from her. And since I'm on my way to her now they've got to hit me someplace between here and the Park East Hotel."

"It sounds worth a try, Glines," he said. "Where are you now?" I gave him the address. "Give me five minutes to get somebody at each end of the line," he said. "How much of a chance are you willing to take?"

"Don't worry. I'll give them as much a chance at me as you'll need."

"Okay, mister. It's your party and good luck."

My watch showed two minutes past nine. The next time I looked at it it was four minutes past. I got up and climbed back into my coat. The .38 went into the outside righthand pocket. At five minutes past I turned out the light, lit a cigarette. My hand was fairly steady with the match but the cigarette was tasteless. Worse than tasteless. Then it was time to leave.

I stood on the sidewalk and acted like a man searching for a cab. There were people out. Some passed behind me and kept walking. Others were dark shapes on the other side of the street. None slowed his pace, none even noticed me. An empty cab, its roof light glowing orange, came down the block and slowed at sight of me. I let it go by. I turned then and strolled toward the avenue, some ninety feet east.

He came from nowhere at all. One moment he wasn't there and the next he was, a squat man with his collar up, his hat down, and a gun in his hand that opened fire from less than thirty feet. But only the first shot was aimed at me and I felt no impact. The rest were not even close—made that way from his shock at being fired upon from three different directions. They came almost simultaneously and I tell you it was a hell of a noisy five seconds.

Then it was over as two plainclothes cops wrestled him to the sidewalk, broke the gun out of his fingers and held him motionless on the pavement with his arms and legs outstretched.

"You all right?" asked a third one, coming up from behind me, his .32 still in his fingers.

"I think so," I told him. "He let one go right at my head. I don't know how the hell he missed."

"I do," he said, and I saw he was a roundfaced man about my own age. "You must have pulled your head down into your chest. The damn slug whistled right past my ear."

We were standing above the trio on the sidewalk.

"How is he?" I asked.

"He says he's hit in the leg," answered the cop holding his shoulders flat. "Some shooting. A dozen tries and one hit."

"That's nothing," I told him. "I didn't even get mine out of my pocket."

I knelt down. The guy who tried to kill me now stared straight into my face expressionlessly and silently.

"Where's St. George?" I asked him softly.

"Go to hell," he said. Then, turning to the detective leaning on his chest, "I want a doctor," he demanded.

"He's already on his way, punk. We think of everything."

I didn't wait around for the ambulance but went in search of a cab that would take me to Kyle. She opened the door quickly—too damn quickly—and was in my arms before I crossed the threshold.

"I thought you'd *never* get here," she murmured, fastening her body to mine from chest to thighs.

I eased her slowly inside, held her with one arm and closed the door and locked it with the other hand.

"Kiss me," she said and I did, fighting to keep a part of my mind aware that there were other things to do before this. "What's the matter, darling?" she asked, holding my face between her soft hands, not lessening the urgent press of her body.

"The phone call," I reminded her.

"Oh, damn the phone call! Only good things can happen to me now that you're here." She pulled my head down impetuously and her lips parted as they met mine. We stood there I don't know how long, swaying slowly, making no sound, hardly breathing. I felt the warmth of her washing me from head to foot and I know that she was telling me it hadn't been like this before.

The telephone was ringing. How long I'll never know.

"No," she said.

"Yes," I said, turning her gently around. "Answer it. It may be good news."

I walked her to the phone with my arm on her waist.

"Hello," she said, her voice hardly more than a whisper. Then her eyebrows went up. "Yes, Captain. He is." She handed the receiver to me with a puzzled expression.

It was Fred Weaver's boss again, his voice infectiously happy.

"It's all over, Glines. We got 'em."

"Nice."

"Can you imagine what that damn fool had in his pockets? A room key to the Leewood Hotel! A *room* key!"

"Who said you had to be smart to steal?"

He laughed. "And who said you had to be smart to catch 'em? But say," he added, his voice going sympathetic, "I'm afraid you made yourself an enemy down at West 20th."

"What did he say?"

"I called him," said the Captain, "and told him to come on down to Centre Street if he wanted to talk to his suspects. Maybe I laid it on a little thick," he admitted, "but we don't often get a chance like this to bring that Homicide Squad down to earth."

"I guess not," I said to be saying something.

"And I told him what you'd done for us," he went on. "From what he called you, Glines, I think you'd better go off on a vacation for a little while."

"Maybe I will, Captain. Have you had a chance to talk to those birds at all?"

"Just to say hello. They're being booked downstairs now, as a matter of fact."

"How many are there?"

"Counting the one at Bellevue, four. The whole mob."

"Fine," I said. "And thanks for calling."

When he rang off I held my finger on the cradle bar for a moment. Then I asked the desk to get me the Leewood Hotel. Some seconds later I was talking to the telephone operator—the recent excitement still echoing in her voice.

"This is the police again," I lied.

"Yessir."

"We have information that a long distance call was made to that room sometime today. Who made the call and where did it come from?" I hoped I sounded good and official.

Apparently I did. "I meant to tell you about that," she said shakily. "I was going to as soon as I had a free minute . . ."

"Tell me now," I said.

"The call came from Brownsville, Texas," she blurted. "But it was station-to-station, no name."

"All right," I said. "Don't give out that information to anyone else."

"I won't," she promised.

That was that. Archie St. George was moving fast. I laid the phone down and turned to find Kyle looking at me strangely.

"They've got them," I said.

She nodded her head, her eyes continuing to search for something in my face.

"All but Archie," I said. "And the police may never learn about him."

"Why?" she asked, in a voice that said she didn't particularly care to know.

"Because the mob needs a friend on the outside. He can help them a lot more out of prison than in with them. Especially a smart friend like Archie. A man with cards to play."

"Oh. And you just found out where Archie is?"

"Yes, Kyle."

"What are you going to do?"

"I'm going to find him. I gave him a chance to be decent yesterday. I can see him laughing when you went back and told him he was free to leave Palm Beach.

He's got your pictures, Kyle, and he's going to use them. He never meant to do anything else."

"It doesn't matter any more," she said. "I don't care what he does with them."

"Yes you do. They'll plague you the way blackmail makes a living hell out of life for thousands of people. Everywhere you go, wherever you try to find happiness— the pictures will turn up in one form or another. They'll be sent in the mail to people you know. High school kids will be able to buy them in the back of the corner candy store."

"I don't care, Barney," she said quietly. "I'll have you. I'll trade Archie the pictures for you."

"Suppose you did. What about me?"

"I don't understand . . ."

"What kind of man would you be getting who'd let another man do that to his wife? Why do you think I didn't ask you to marry me yesterday morning? Or today? Or tonight?"

She had her eyes closed. "Yes. You'd be searching for him the rest of our lives, wouldn't you?"

"I couldn't promise anything else. Not and be the same man you told me you fell in love with."

She nodded and then turned abruptly toward the arch. I listened to the sound of her feet echoing along the long hallway. Then it was silent. I picked up the telephone. "No more calls tonight," I said and set it down slowly.

She stood in the center of the rose-walled bedroom, the soft glow of the two lamps bathing her breathtaking nakedness in a dark red tone.

I carried her to the bed.

Afterwards I noticed something atop the dresser that had not been there when I had come to her before. It was the picture of Archie St. George.

"Why?" I asked.

"Last night," she said, her eyes closed. "I had to get it out of my mind. Out of me."

"Was it bad?"

"It was bad, Barney. But there's nothing left of it. I put his picture there while you were outside. I looked at it and all I remembered of Archie was as he had been." She turned on her side, reaching her hand toward my face. "You made it never happen."

We were both relaxed now, aware of each other and not ourselves.

"Put out your light," she whispered, reaching over to turn hers off. "I have the feeling I'm being watched." Her voice was rich and happy-sounding. It came to me next in the dark. "I have a feeling I want to be wicked," she said.

TWELVE

We ate the breakfast next morning rather quietly. Kyle picked up the few dishes and took them out of the room. I caught up with her in the little kitchen, my hands circling her long slim waist.

"What do you have to do today?" I asked her.

She lifted my hands. "Rehearse a television show at eleven," she said, swaying to some music she seemed to be hearing. "I can postpone it."

"No. I have to get down to my office. Can you meet me downtown at two?"

"Downtown where?"

"City Hall, Kyle. Marriage bureau."

"Let me think about it for a second," she murmured. Then she turned to face me. "Are you sure that's what you want, Barney? You don't have to."

"Either do you. I'm the one who's asking you to."

"I'm the one accepting." She glanced beyond me. "Look at the time!" she cried. "Ten-thirty! Come on," she said, taking my hand and pulling me along, "help me get dressed."

"You are dressed," I pointed out.

"This is a dramatic show," she said. "I've got to get into something snaky."

It was. A white gown that didn't begin until halfway down her chest and clung to her like another skin.

"What happens to you in this drama?" I asked.

"The villain throws me to the floor twice," she said, grinning into the mirror. "And we have a wild struggle in his penthouse. The rest of the time I'm just walking and sitting. And being made violent love to," she added.

114

Then she whirled around and was in my arms. "Not like this, though," she said later. "It isn't allowed." I walked with her to the door.

"I feel slightly ridiculous," I admitted, "seeing you off to work."

Her eyes searched mine earnestly. "It won't be that kind of marriage, Barney. This one's going to click."

"I'm not worrying about it."

"Don't get all involved at your office. Don't keep me waiting at the church."

"The license bureau," I said.

"Till two," she said and I watched her stride away down the corridor.

I finished my own dressing thoughtfully, wondering what it was going to be like married. Give and take, my friends tell me. Compromise, they say, and there are no problems. Well, I was compromising on something, I thought, studying Archie St. George's picture. If I wanted Kyle I had to take him along with her.

But not for long—and maybe soon enough to keep him from doing anything with his shakedown. I was sure Weaver's boss would put a warrant out for him. Then the FBI could take over from there on a state's-line fugitive charge. With all the help I could throw their way.

I had my tie knotted when the doorbell sounded. It was the desk clerk.

"This came special delivery for Miss Shannon," he said, his face set primly, his bespectacled eyes gazing right through me as he handed a small flat package into my hand.

I thanked him hollowly and shut the door. I had seen the postmark, "Brownsville, Texas." I carried it out in front of me to the small table that held her father's portrait and set it down as though it might explode. I stood there staring at the postmark, the scripted name and address, the shape of the package. My eyes travelled to something behind the picture-frame. It was a long-bladed, bone-handled knife. On the handle was an engraved metal strip. I picked it up.

The engraving said: "To my baby. In my day a weapon, in hers a letter-opener. Good! From her Dad." I hefted it, half my mind on the character of the man who'd had such an inscription made, half my mind on the package from Texas. The tumbling thought joined.

"What would you do for your daughter, Shannon? You've got the face of a man I'd like to have known. What would you do about somebody named Archie St. George?"

The knife balanced in my palm just below the handle. In his day it was a weapon. In my day a .38 was a weapon and this thing I held was a letter-opener, just as a man had wished for his daughter. I took it and slashed violently at the wrappings on the little package

The paper came away to reveal four playing cards, the four queens, face up. Folded beneath them was a note.

"This little item looks like a sure-fire seller. You can have it—exclusively—for fifty grand. Somebody will be in touch with you, if they haven't already. Give my best to the sucker." It wasn't signed.

I turned the queen of spades over. On its back was a picture of Kyle, two inches by three inches, modeling a small hat, her body naked. What I had seen in this same bedroom last night—what had been the beginning and the end of everything I was living for—was now an obscenity on the back of a playing card.

I saw the deck—the fifty-two of them in the hands of thousands and thousands of men playing gin and canasta and poker—or just matching cards, backs up—plus the other tens of thousands who didn't need gambling with their perversion.

I saw the calendars, twelve inches by sixteen inches, hanging in every garage and off-street barber shop, taking the place of honor in every dormitory room from Princeton to Southern Cal. I saw the postcards, the flip-

books, the "sunbathing" magazines, the "girl-of-the-
month" picture clubs.

I was looking into the steady, unwavering glance of
Kyle's father and I knew goddamned well what he would
have done.

She'd be at the license bureau at two. She'd sit there,
terribly embarrassed, hurt, until three. But I needed the
time. She mustn't know where I was.

But she had to know why we weren't going to be married. Not yet. I took the wrapping paper, tore the postmark out, shoved it into my pocket, shredded the cards,
left them in a pile on the table and left the hotel.

THIRTEEN

I ARRIVED in Brownsville with three thousand dollars—all I had in the world—and began spending it immediately. A '49 Olds, registered to Albert Worthen of Bridgeport, Connecticut, took eleven hundred of it. Forty dollars got me a room for four weeks in advance and another fifty bought the white suit and accessories. I put the clothes I'd arrived in into a closet, locked the door, and started looking for Archie St. George.

Where? In bars. Small bars, big bars, dark bars, bright bars. Buy a highball and drink it off. Buy a second and nurse it, speaking to no one, keeping to myself. Then, when he was nearby and doing nothing particular, bracing the bartender casually.

Would he know a man was from New York just by looking at him? Sure, he'd smile. You're from New York yourself. Had he seen another one today, or yesterday? Good-looking guy, early thirties, six feet.

The fifth place I hit made him. Archie had come in early in the afternoon and been half-carried, half-pushed out at two in the morning. The bartender didn't know which direction he took when he reached the street and didn't care.

"He was a loudmouth," I was told. "Couldn't hold his liquor."

I left and turned right. Two blocks away was a green neon sign, "Rooms." I described St. George all over again.

"You and me both, mister! That tinhorn jumped his bill! Carried him upstairs early this morning and the cleaning lady found him gone at eleven. You a friend of his?"

"Not especially," I said, but I handed over five dollars to keep Archie from being picked up on that charge before I reached him.

It was also information well paid for. If Archie had the shorts so bad he had to risk a vagrancy arrest for five dollars, his trail should get simpler to follow. And where could he live if two-fifty a night was steep?

I crossed into Mexico at two-thirty the next morning and slept until noon in a place called the Hotel Amigo, a motel setup along the big highway. And for the next fourteen days I drove and walked and drank and slept and ate—and drove. Four thousand miles piled up on the speedometer and five hundred dollars dwindled from my stake without so much as a doubtful hint about Archie St. George.

Then it occurred to me. He had waited another day after sending the first package of pictures, maybe two. Then another set had gone north to Kyle, a variation on what could be done with the poses. Had she wired him the money, warned him to get far away? I had to know how things stood, how far they had gone. But most of all, I think, I wanted to hear Kyle's voice again.

I was driving through a town. Not a town but a small cluster of wooden buildings. On my left was a sleepy little bar. Across the street was a Mexican version of a general store and post office. A small sign read "Teléfono" and I pulled in.

I wrote out my name for the woman inside, along with Kyle's and the number of the Park East Hotel. Then I waited. Twenty-five minutes went by when she said, "Okay, meester. You call is ready."

The "telephone booth" was a doorless partition whose one side was part of the store window. I stepped into it and held the old fashioned receiver to my ear, feeling like a goldfish.

"Mr. Glines?" said a crisp-voiced operator.

"Yes."

"We have the Park East Hotel in New York City, sir. But Miss Kyle Shannon is not there at the moment."

"Can you ask them when to expect . . . Never mind," I said and let the receiver fall on its hook. Across the street a man in brown slacks and a sport jacket had entered the bar, the *La Cantada*. It was the same outfit I had seen enter a cab in Palm Beach. I'd found Archie St. George.

I went over to the woman at the counter. Stuck beneath the base of her local phone was the piece of paper with my name on it.

I looked at the shelves behind her.

"Yes?" she asked, struggling with the simple English word, giving it three syllables.

"Cigarettes," I said. She turned to get them and I recovered the paper.

I paid for them. "Forget the call," I said, shaking my head. "No *teléfono*." Then I slipped out of the door and went hunting for wherever it was St. George was living.

That was easy. There was one hotel in the town, a town called Tia Rosa. Through the open doorway I could see a fat, blackhaired desk clerk idly reading a paper. I saw him yawn twice within five minutes.

I turned and walked in the opposite direction from the bar. Soon I was all out of houses and on a dirt road. Off the road, on a trail just wide enough for a car, was a leanto.

I circled Tia Rosa's business district completely, coming to the general store from the opposite direction. I started the Olds as quietly as I could and eased it away and back toward the leanto.

When I looked into the hotel again the clerk was asleep. I went past him and climbed the stairs to the floor above. There were six doors along the hallway. Two of them were locked. I entered one of the unlocked rooms that looked down on the street. It was empty.

In the adjoining door was a key. I turned it and

found myself in a whiskey-reeking shambles that could only belong to St. George. That I got to work.

The negatives and various-sized prints were in the fourth place I looked—rolled into the space behind the baseplug in the wall. With them I found two Post Office receipts. One from the package I had intercepted from Brownsville, the other from Texas City. It was dated ten days ago and suggested that Archie might have entered Mexico by boat.

I put the pictures into my jacket, replaced the plug and went back to 'my' room to wait. I had no sooner closed the connecting door when I heard him lurching down the hall.

I decided to wait until it got dark. I heard Archie starting in with the bottles. Drink hearty, Archie. Bottoms up, you son of a bitch, you're drinking your last.

I didn't move for a whole hour, not even to light a cigarette. I even breathed through my mouth.

Okay, Archie. Drink up. I can't wait to see your face.

FOURTEEN

"No MORE TALK, baby."

It was a girl's voice, complaining, wheedling. I stirred and opened my eyes. I was in a room, on a bed. I wore a shirt and stained white trousers and no shoes. On the table was a whiskey bottle, empty, and two dirty-looking glasses.

"You ready now, baby?"

Ready for what? I felt like hell. I couldn't remember seeing this girl before, and I wasn't ready for anything. My mind was filled with a vague, jumbled impression of what had happened back in Tia Rosa. The stifling room, St. George, and then Kyle. . . . Kyle, and, finally, Archie St. George's dead body. I had got the hell out of there, fast. But then . . . then what?

"I ask you, baby, you ready now?"

She was beside me, coming to a kneeling position on the bed as I turned my eyes to her, hovering over me. Black, jet black, hair hung to her shoulders, shining in the light from the bulb directly overhead. Her face was very thin, very young, and her lower lip was set in a sultry expression.

"Who are you?" I asked, and was shocked at the hoarseness, the dead-tiredness of my voice.

Her lips smiled but her dark eyes snapped angrily. "No more games," she said, and I realized she spoke with a Mexican accent. "You want Lily or not?"

I shook my head. It felt as though it would burst from the pain inside.

"Yes!" she said, moving closer to me.

I pushed her aside and tried to sit up.

"Tuu! I spit on your bitch!" She stood on the floor, hands on her hips, her face wild and in that moment terribly ugly. She spat again. "Kyle!" She whirled around the bed to a chair that held clothes. "Talk, talk, talk!" she screamed at me. A dress was pulled over her head swiftly. She jammed her tiny feet into high-heeled shoes and fastened the straps. "Go find your Kyle bitch, you drunken American pig!" she said furiously, going to the door of the room.

"Wait!" I was on my feet, swaying unsteadily.

"Go to hell!"

She had to stay and tell me.

"Where am I?" I asked her.

She laughed. A piercing sound that throbbed in my head. "Where *are* you?"

I didn't say anything.

"You in Camargo, where you think?"

I could only shake my head and stare at her.

"My God! I know you plenty drunk tonight . . ." Her face softened suddenly and her voice became questioning. "Don't you know where you are?"

She came toward me slowly, her head set to one side quizzically. "This is Camargo," she told me, making an explanation. "You been here week now."

"A week?"

She stood below me, nodding seriously. "I see you in bar downstairs every night," she said. "But you don't see me until tonight. You buy me drink and call me Kyle." She stopped and waited, searching my face carefully.

Only the name meant anything. Everything.

"You remember now?"

"No." I looked around. My jacket was on the bare floor and I went to it slowly and picked it up. The wallet was inside and I drew it up. "Can I give you something?"

"You got nothing to give," she told me. "You broke."

"Oh."

She shrugged her shoulders. "Serve me damn good,"

she said. "I gonna be your sweetheart tonight because you look like good guy but broke." Then her sadness dropped away. "Listen! You feel pretty lousy now, no? Lily be right back with beans. You like tamale? Fix you up good. Make you strong in the legs."

"I don't want to eat. Do I still have a car?"

"In garage," she told me. "They keep it till you pay for fixing."

I nodded. I remembered a lot of it now.

"You stay right here," she said. "Lily be back in five, ten minutes."

She left me and I went over and sat down on the edge of the bed. Only when my head was bent forward, propped by my arms, did some of the pain subside. But that was no good. The less it throbbed the more I was able to think.

There had been no sight of Kyle by the time I reached the street. I ran all the way to the leanto, cursing the distance and the darkness. I got the car on the road and sent it hurtling along the road Kyle had taken. It was not the highway, but a narrow, twisting dirt road not quite wide enough for two cars. Suddenly it began to climb and the turns became sharper, more numerous. I had the throttle to the floorboard and both hands struggled with the wheel to keep from leaving the road.

Then, at the end of a hairpin curve, I was jamming my foot against the brake pedal but not in time to miss smashing the horse and cart. Even as I hit I saw the tangled, still-smoking wreck of the other car.

I climbed from the Olds painfully to be met by an old Mexican. I remembered that tears were streaming down his cheeks and his eyes were wide with horror. I stumbled past him toward the overturned convertible, fell to my knees and tried to crawl through the squashed opening that had been the window. But there was no one inside!

I got to my feet to find the old man pointing a badly shaking arm down the side of the rocky hill below the road. His mouth opened and closed but no words came past his shocked lips.

I went down the hill, unable to keep my footing, letting myself slide through the blackness. It took a quarter of an hour to find her, wedged between two gray boulders, her arms and legs flung out grotesquely. There was no life.

I think I took her in my arms and brought her, somehow, to the road again. I can't be sure of that. It might be something I did, or it might be something I wished I had done.

This was Camargo? I've been here a week? I don't remember. I don't know what happened to me after I saw Kyle, I don't care.

She had loved me and had come to Tia Rosa and killed Archie St. George to keep his blood off my hands. Daughter of a man named Shannon, she fought her own battles.

I climbed to my feet and got over to my shoes. I put them on and then the jacket. Did I still own a hat? Who cares? There was no money in my wallet. Who cares? All that was important was to get out of here before that girl came back. If she ever made me strong enough I might kill her.

The door burst open on me. Lily stood there, her dark eyes blazing. Behind her were two Mexicans. Soldiers, I thought at first, but then recognized them as Federal police. They pushed her aside and came into the room.

But I wasn't watching *them*. My eyes were all for the man in the American-blue suit and the New York hat. It was Stern.

"Hello, Glines," he said.

"Hello, Lieutenant."

"I'm going to take you home," he said.

"Home? I did nothing in New York."

"I didn't say that."

"St. George was killed here," I said. "It's their murder."

"They think they know all about it," he said. "They don't want you." He stepped toward me, holding an envelope in his hand. "They found this in her car," he said.

It was addressed to the New York City Police. I read:

"This is being written in the village of Tia Rosa, State of Tamaulipas, Mexico. I have come here to murder a man named Archie St. George of New York who had been blackmailing me. I alone am responsible for this crime. No one else is involved. Signed, Kyle Shannon."

I folded it and gave it back to him.

"She's what it was all about, wasn't she, Glines?"

"Yes," I said, "she was."

He put his hand under my arm as though to steady me.

"You'll get over it," he said. "It'll take a little while, but you'll get over it."

"Sure," I heard myself saying. "It'll take a little while."